Who

The white car door opened and a tall man with broad shoulders got out. The sun blazed down on his tousled blond hair. As he walked toward my window, he stretched out both arms like he had been driving a long time without a rest. . . . My mouth fell open, just watching him. Nobody that handsome had ever pulled into Romney, not since I was born. . . . That man was so good-looking, it was almost sinful.

Other Point paperbacks
you will enjoy:

Until Whatever
by Martha Humphreys

Storm Rising
by Marilyn Singer

Sheila's Dying
by Alden Carter

Life Without Friends
by Ellen Emerson White

point

The Brightest Light

COLLEEN O'SHAUGHNESSY McKENNA

SCHOLASTIC INC.
New York   Toronto   London   Auckland   Sydney

ISBN 0-590-45348-3

12 11 10 9 8 7 6 5 4 3 2 1   10   4 5 6 7 8 9/9

Printed in the U.S.A.   01

This book is dedicated
with special thanks to my mother,
Ruth Short Shaughnessy, and her loving family
in Romney, West Virginia, and to my husband, Jay,
who is my brightest light.

The Brightest Light

It's so early the birds sound as if they are in charge of the world. I've been staring out the window for hours, watching threads of pink stretch across the sky, wondering if I made the right decision. I've been thinking so hard on things lately that all the black and white of life has blurred into a gray fog; a fog so thick you feel safe till you realize you left the main road a long time ago, and now you're falling off a cliff headfirst.

It's been a headfirst kind of summer.

The sun's shooting through my window now, and the birds are quiet as they scatter and start doing whatever it is birds do in the last hot days of August in Romney, West Virginia. I'd better get going, too. My Gramma Belle says that I never start anything at the beginning, but now I have to. It's important to say it right. Maybe the facts will fall into some sort of order, and the sense of what has happened to me will rise to the top like morning cream.

I'll start with my first week at Jake's and work my way through the summer.

Chapter One

Jake's Dairy Queen has been in need of a fresh coat of paint for as long as I can remember. The bike stand out front is so rusty, nobody in his right mind wants his bike anywhere near it. Half the signs taped to the windows are faded pale from the sun, making it hard to tell which picture is of a banana split and which is of a fried clam platter. None of that really matters though. Jake's is still the most popular place to be during the sticky, hot days of summer in Romney, West Virginia. Jake's gives the old people a turnaround place for their walks, and the high school kids come down to see who's after whom. So, of course, I was real pleased when Jake asked me to be his window girl for the summer. I've been saving up for a secondhand car to use my senior year, so the prospect of making steady money was nice.

Jake does the cooking, which really isn't all that much. He deep-fries fish squares, lays out hot

1

dogs on his rolling machine, and makes three or four gallons of his spicy sloppy Joes in a big black pot. I take care of the cones, shakes, and Dilly bars. The only bad part of the job is wearing the orange-and-brown-checked uniforms his mother-in-law made two summers ago.

"You're a good worker, Kitty Lee," Jake said my very first week. "You hand out those cones faster than anyone I ever saw."

I smiled, glad to know I was doing a good job.

"Yep," Jake continued, hollering above the whine of the can opener. "You hand out them cones faster than a Las Vegas slot machine spitting out nickels."

My smile was pretty near ear to ear. If I had had a tail, I probably would have wagged it.

Jake emptied another can of stewed tomatoes into the pot. "Give me one hardworking Kitty Lee Carter instead of ten of them beauty queens they got lifeguarding down at community pool, any day."

My eyes narrowed, wishing I could zap Jake right into the walk-in freezer. You'd think a man his age would know when to stop talking. I try not to let Jake's teasing get to me. Fact is, I have never had any illusions about being the prettiest girl in school. Nobody once asked me to be the Fourth of July Queen, and boys didn't line up around the block to ask me out on a real Saturday night date. I've been waking up to the same ordinary face for the last sixteen years. Truth is, I am too tall and too thin to be worried about a talent scout chasing me down Main Street begging me to sign up with him.

2

Gramma Belle is forever telling me to count my blessings considering I started out life all scrawny and red-faced. Gramma says I've turned out better than anyone hoped. Luckily I got her bright blue eyes and Pop's thick black curly hair and eyelashes. Everyone in Romney tells me I've got my momma's turned-up nose. Momma was so tiny, I suppose on her the nose looked cute. On me it looks like God just got tired and reached in the button jar and sewed one on in a hurry. Momma was only five foot one and knock-down gorgeous. I wish we had more pictures of her around the house. The only one around is on my dresser. It's a great picture with Momma sitting on the back of Pop's car with her legs crossed and her head flung back so her hair flowed down her back like a shiny blonde waterfall.

When I ask my Pop why we don't have more pictures of Momma setting around the house, he says that pictures won't bring her back. Answers like that don't answer a thing. Momma died when I was two, barely old enough to remember more than the fact I loved her. I had to go all the way up in the attic to get the one picture for my bedroom. It was in a small box with Momma's jewelry. The box was marked "Marjorie" in Pop's small cramped printing. Another box had Momma's oil paints, and a third box had a collection of tiny glass dogs that Gramma Belle said was Momma's pride. I wanted to bring them downstairs so we could all enjoy them, but Gramma just shook her head hard and said, "No, and don't go upsetting your father with mention of them neither." Pop and Gramma seem to have wrapped most every-

3

thing about Momma in small boxes.

In my picture, Momma looks nice. I knew she wasn't on top of that car showing off how pretty she was; she looked shy, pleased someone wanted to take her picture. I wished I had an album all about her and Pop. They got married the very afternoon they graduated high school. I was born seventeen months later and named after Momma's favorite movie star, Katharine Hepburn.

Gramma Belle told me once that Momma was always walking me uptown to show me off. Since I was just a bitty thing, folks snipped my name from Katharine to Kat, and finally to Kitty.

"Hey now, wake up, Kitty! Jake isn't paying you to daydream!"

I blinked into the perfect face of Jessica LaShay. Jessica was sort of the queen of the high school. She was bending down to shout at me through the window, all the while shaking back her mane of thick red hair, knowing that every boy sitting at the picnic tables surrounding the parking lot was smiling at her.

"What do you want, Jessica?"

"Why, don't you look cute in your uniform! And I love that hairnet you're wearing, Kitty," Jessica laughed. "Maybe I can sneak one of my gram's white sparkle nets down for you to wear on the Fourth of July." Jessica shot a smile over her tanned shoulder at the boys.

"You want to order, Jessica?" I asked again, my fingers already itching to stuff a large vanilla cone right in her face.

"Diet soda will be fine," she said. She made a big to-do about inching her fingers into her pocket to get some change. "If I didn't have to get into that bitty dress to wear over at the college dance next Friday, I could treat myself to a cone."

"Fifty cents," I said, setting the soda down with a thump. I didn't offer her a straw. I was watching Jessica walk across the lot, watching the boys watch her, when the fanciest car I ever saw pulled in. It crunched across the loose gravel and stopped two feet from my window. The windows were rolled up, tinted dark, the whitewall tires cleaner than a baby's first pair of white leather shoes. Even the boys from the picnic table stopped watching Jessica and stared openmouthed at the car.

"Glory, would you take a look at that," hooted Jake. He crossed his arms over his huge chest and grinned. "Have to sell a lot of chili dogs to get the keys to that!"

The white car door opened and a tall man with broad shoulders got out. The sun blazed down on his tousled blond hair. As he walked toward my window, he stretched out both arms like he had been driving a long time without a rest. Both cuffs of his white dress shirt were rolled past his wrists, and his gold watch glistened against his tanned arm. My mouth fell open, just watching him. Nobody that handsome had ever pulled into Romney, not since I was born. I kept wiping the counter slowly, not even realizing what I was doing till my dishrag ended up in the bowl of rainbow jimmies. That man was so good-looking, it was almost sinful.

The man turned and pointed to the car. "Stay inside. I'll order."

5

Before he even turned back, the car doors opened and three little kids bolted out. The oldest was a boy about eight, next was a little girl about five years old with tangled brown hair hanging down her back. Stumbling along behind was a tiny little girl who must have been two or three. All three of them were dressed in fancy sun suits, but their faces were dirty and their hair was sticking up all over the place.

The girls raced over to the bike rack, while their brother picked up some stones and flung them into the air, laughing as they fell like hail.

"Three small cones," said the man. His voice was low and smooth, reminding me of what sweet caramel syrup would sound like if it could talk. I glanced up at him, just about to ask if he would like sugar or cake cones, when he slowly pulled off his sunglasses. His eyes were pale blue, the color you wish the sky could always stay.

He grinned at me and repeated his order.

"Cake or . . . sugar?" I stammered. This man was too young to be the daddy of those little kids. Maybe he was just an uncle, or a friend of the family who stopped by to say hello. Maybe he was a college student on his way home.

The man didn't even turn to ask the kids what type of cone they wanted. "Anything's fine."

"It's raining, it's raining," shouted the little boy as he threw more stones into the air.

"Don't, Joey!" cried the older girl. "That hurts!"

Joey bent down and threw another handful.

I got so worried about those kids whooping it up in the parking lot, acting like a bunch of puppies just set free from the kennel, I didn't even

6

ask the man if he wanted chocolate sprinkles or rainbow jimmies on his cones. Any minute now Hank Rollins would come a barreling across the parking lot in his big blue pickup like a bat out of hell for his lunchtime sloppy Joes. Come noontime, Hank was always too hungry to be on the lookout for a passel of little kids racing around the parking lot.

"Mister, you better make those kids go sit on the picnic tables before they get themselves hit by a car."

The man turned, putting his sunglasses back on and staring at the kids like he was seeing them for the first time. As I scooped the ice cream, I studied his profile. With his straight nose and strong chin, he looked just like one of those Greek statues outside the courthouse in Cumberland. I bit my lip so I wouldn't smile. I sure hoped he wasn't their daddy. I could hardly wait to tell my best friend, Dottie Ramsey, about him. Dottie was forever swearing that no handsome men ever came within a fifty-mile radius of Romney.

Jessica was sitting on the hood of her blue Mustang, staring at him and crunching her ice so fast she was liable to freeze off her tongue.

"There's a tire swing over there by the fence," I pointed out. "Those little kids would be better off over there."

Maybe this man was only a visiting relative and didn't know much about kids, didn't realize how fast accidents could happen.

"Look at me," cried the oldest girl. She held out both arms and twirled around like a ballerina inside a jewelry box. "Watch, Daddy!"

7

My thumb crunched into the sugar cone. So he *was* their daddy after all.

"Mister, I hate to tell you your business, but . . ."

"Children, children," called out the man in a low, smooth voice. His voice must have been soaked right up by the heat, never reaching those kids, 'cause the next second they took off again in three different directions.

Gramma Belle tells me I have a real irritating habit of making everyone else's business my own. She says I should work on stopping it quick before I don't have a friend left in the world. But I couldn't just stand there and watch a bit of a girl pelting a bike stand with rocks. It was Gramma herself who told me about Monty Blake. Monty was barely five when he shot a rock at the side of a diner, too young to duck when it came boomeranging right back at him and took out his left eye.

I snatched up all three cones in my hand, bumping open the screen door with my hip, and marched outside.

"Hey now," I said in the cheerful voice I use when I help Gramma Belle teach one of her Sunday school classes. "Come on over here by the tables and I'll give you each an ice cream cone."

The boy raced right up to me. He was frowning. "Give me mine."

"Up on the bench first," I said, holding the cone out of his reach. I smiled at the littlest girl, already climbing up on the bench. She grinned at me and reached up with both hands for her cone.

"Chrissy, get off that bench," ordered the boy. "It has bird poop all over it."

"It's dirty," agreed the middle girl, pushing back her mass of hair. She stood next to her brother and stared up at me.

Out of the corner of my eye I could see the man walking quickly across the lot to us. Good, he could come and make them mind. I already had three people backed up at the window, jingling their change and watching.

"Daddy, make this girl give us our ice cream," the little boy cried.

"She made Chrissy sit on bird poop," added his sister.

"Y'all should sit down before you get yourself killed by a car," I said with a big smile. I hoped my smile didn't look too fake like one of those toothpaste ads. Truth was, I didn't feel like smiling one bit. You would think kids coming out of such a nice car would have better manners.

The man took the cones right out of my hands and passed them on to the kids. He didn't even look at me, just kind of acted like I was some sort of ice cream vending machine.

"Bradley, I'm waiting!"

We all turned and stared at the blonde head sticking out of the white Mercedes. As soon as I saw her, I knew right off that the handsome man was married to her. She looked like one of those soap opera stars. Most of her face was covered up with her huge black glasses, but the part that was showing was beautiful. She tapped her long red fingernails against the side mirror. "For crying out loud, let's get going," she snapped. She drew her head back in and the tinted window rolled back up.

The kids stopped licking for a minute, then turned their backs on the car. The man shoved his hands deep into his pockets and stared at the ground.

"I could stick those cones in a plastic cup for you," I offered. "Then you could take them in the car." I glanced quickly up at his face. "Then your wife won't have to wait."

The man shook his head. "No, thanks." He took off his sunglasses and rubbed his hand over his eyes.

"At least let me give you some extra napkins then," I suggested, turning to leave. His wife seemed mad enough without three dripping cones on the leather car seats.

The man reached out and stopped me by the arm. "We have enough; we'll be fine." He pressed a five-dollar bill into my hand and smiled at me. "Keep the change. You've been great."

I shook my head, holding back the five dollars. "It's too big of a tip, mister," I started to say.

But he had already set out across the parking lot in long, even strides, his eyes hidden behind the dark glasses and his three little kids trailing behind him like chickens.

Chapter Two

Things were so busy the rest of the day, I didn't have time to think about the family in the Mercedes. Part of me was disappointed that the handsome man with the pale blue eyes was a married man and a daddy of three, but another part of me felt something wasn't quite right with that group.

The later it got, the more I glanced up at the clock. It was Saturday night and I wanted to keep ahead of things, sponging up any spills right away so that I could bolt early and walk up to the Regent Theater with Dottie. The Regent only has one Saturday matinee and one evening show a week, but that's enough to host half of Romney. Folks with little kids go to the matinee, because they know that the evening show will be full up with couples on dates, with the rest of the audience wishing hard that they had one.

Dottie and I usually had more fun without a

11

date. We'd been going to the Saturday night movie together since seventh grade and trusted each other not to desert the other just because some fool boy out by the concession stand wanted to go upstairs and make out in the balcony.

Dottie never had a steady boyfriend, but she always had a date for the Christmas dance and big events at the high school. She was very pretty, but a tad on the heavy side, which scared off some of the boys.

My Gramma Belle loves Dottie and was forever asking her to stay for supper. Gramma said cooking for Dottie was pure joy because Dottie almost glowed after a good meal. But Dottie likes people a lot more than food. She never said a mean word against anyone, never once.

I was in the middle of a banana split when she started knocking hard on the side window. "Kitty Lee. Hi! Listen, I have to talk to you!"

I nodded and held up a scoop of ice cream to let her know I was tied up at the moment.

"Kitty, don't wait for me after work." Dottie stuck her hand through the opening and knocked on the counter. "I'm going to have to cancel — "

"Miss, I don't *want* cherries," shouted the elderly lady on the other side of the window. She scrunched down low and hollered it again through the window like I couldn't hear straight. "Take those cherries off, dear. Cherries give me gas."

"Okay, no cherries," I called back, wondering if I should forget the nuts, too.

"The little girl who worked here last summer always gave me extra napkins," explained the lady

12

as she pulled thick bundles from the dispenser. "I keep them in my purse."

Dottie knocked again. "Listen, Kitty Lee, I've got to run. I can't go to the movies with you tonight."

"Hey, get to the back of the line, Dottie!" yelled Lester. He yanked Dottie out of line by her shirttail and started laughing.

"You keep your hands off me, Lester Johnston," Dottie laughed. "I'll call you tomorrow, Kitty."

"A double chocolate cone," Lester called out.

"Dottie, what came up?" I asked, reaching to get a cone. But by the time I'd turned around, Dottie was gone.

Dottie and I hadn't missed a Saturday movie in years, so I felt a little odd, like someone left on the dance floor in the middle of a song. Just then Hank Rollins showed up at Jake's, laying on his horn as he and his dogs pulled into the parking lot. By the time Hank ordered his usual five sloppy Joes, I got real busy. As soon as the line disappeared, I scrubbed out the sink and watched the hot dogs twirling slowly around on the rotisserie. No matter how many times those wieners rolled, they stayed right where they were. On certain days living in Romney was exactly that way. Plenty of footwork and not a mile to show for it.

By the time I took care of the customers coming off a Trailways bus, it was time to start cleaning up. I turned on the front yellow bug lights and started sweeping the cement walk. It was almost eight and Mrs. Hawkins was due any minute to work till eleven. Her husband was laid up with a stroke in their front room and she needed a little income till he was back on his feet.

I leaned against my broom, smelling the honeysuckle growing off to the side. Summer felt and smelled, so good. I started to hose down the walk, scattering cigarette butts off into the gravel, and wondering if it was too early to wash off the picnic tables. Since Dottie couldn't meet me for the movie, I wondered if maybe I should skip it tonight and go home and read on the porch with Pop and Gramma Belle. I could stop for some pretzels and soda and make a party out of it. Maybe Pop wouldn't go to bed so early if I stayed home. He was sleeping too much lately. Pop said it was the summer heat, but it was more than that. For the past couple of weeks he had been acting tired, like he was bored stiff with life.

"Get up!"

A little girl's scream scared me so much I dropped the hose. I quickly twisted the water off, then turned and wiped my eyes, staring at the commotion across the street.

"Watch where you're going!" shrieked a woman. She reached down and yanked at the little girl's arm like she was a yo-yo.

"Don't," cried the little girl, pulling back her arms and wrapping them tightly around her chest. "No, Momma!"

" 'No, Momma!' " mimicked the lady. Then the lady turned and started walking fast. At first the little girl ran after her, but after a few yards she stopped and sat down on the curb, crying harder than ever.

"Hey, are you okay, honey?" I called out. I didn't

want to rush up to her and scare her more. I stopped and looked down the sidewalk, waiting for the mother to come running back. Maybe she was just trying to scare her little girl. I didn't want to get in the middle of anything.

When the little girl's cries didn't stop, I hurried across the street. The little girl looked up at me, wiping her face with the backs of her hands.

"Hey, don't cry, honey. My name is Kitty Lee. I work at the ice cream stand across the street. Do you want me to call somebody?" I asked gently. I stopped five feet from the little girl. She looked so tiny, maybe only five or six years old.

"Get my daddy," she said softly.

Before I could ask her name, I heard footsteps and shouting. A tall man, followed by two small children, raced down the sidewalk. As he came closer I recognized him — he was the man from the white Mercedes. I took a few steps back, feeling like some sort of peeping Tom.

"Daddy," cried the little girl, scrambling up from the sidewalk and running toward him. "Mommy's mad at me!"

The man swung her up in his arms. "Janice, Daddy's here." He rubbed her back and kissed her wet cheeks.

I wiped my hands on my orange-and-brown-checked skirt and turned back to the Dairy Queen. I was embarrassed for the man and his kids. What was eating his wife, anyway? Things were racing around inside of me and I couldn't catch hold of one of them. There was something downright scary about a grown woman turning on her own like that. Sure, I didn't have a momma to fuss over

15

me, but at least I didn't have a momma to fuss *at* me.

"Thank you," the man called out as I started across the street.

I turned back. "I . . . is your little girl okay?" I finally asked.

The man nodded. Even in the shadows I could see the shame on his face. Right now he looked a lot older. Maybe I should have stayed in the shadows, letting him think the whole ugly scene had gone unnoticed by strangers.

"She's okay," he said quietly. He reached down and took the little girl's hand. "Janice, come on. Let's go home and finish our game of Candyland. It's almost bedtime."

At the corner, the man turned, his eyes meeting mine. I started to raise my hand and wave, to let him know I didn't think any of this meanness was part of his doing. But he just turned and headed down Locust Street. Nobody looked back. So it was just me, standing there, my hand frozen in a lonely salute.

Chapter Three

Within ten minutes, every moth and mosquito in Romney had arrived at Jake's, thick as locusts, batting themselves silly against the neon lights. Mrs. Hawkins ran in, her sweater pulled over her head like a hood.

"Lord have mercy! Kitty Lee, turn off the outside lights for a minute. I thought I was going to be eaten alive."

I flicked off the lights and we both giggled and counted to thirty. Since it was getting late, I figured unless another Trailways bus went past, we wouldn't lose too many customers. As soon as I turned the switch back on and heard the hum of lights, I said good night to Mrs. Hawkins.

Outside, my footsteps crunched across the gravel, loud as tap shoes on a church floor. Gazing out across the parking lot, I looked at where the Mercedes family had been. I wasn't quite sure of what I could have said to them face to face. It was

17

always embarrassing to see someone's bad side before you saw their good.

I walked down Maple Street, running my fingertips against hedges and fence palings, trying to decide what to do with my night. Gramma Belle and Pop wouldn't be expecting me home for another three hours since they thought I was going to the show with Dottie.

Somehow, reading on the porch didn't seem too interesting anymore. It was too sticky a night, the bugs were bad, and after a long day of standing on my feet, I guess I wanted to just sit down and be entertained. Everyone went to the Regent on Saturday. I was sure to catch up with someone to sit with.

As I turned onto First Street, I could see a crowd of kids from school gathered around the Foodway. The Regent sells candy and popcorn, but they charge so much that most kids just stop at the Foodway to buy their Milky Ways and Milk Duds. Course, first-time daters usually splurge at the concession stand. A kid just starting out wouldn't want to be branded as a cheapskate.

"Hey, well, look who's here! Don't you look cute in your little uniform!"

I grinned. I still couldn't get used to Cody Baines having such a deep rumbling voice. He was my closest friend next to Dottie. Time was when Cody and I were *best* friends. Cody's mother knew my momma before she died, so Mrs. Baines always tried to keep an eye on me. But it was Cody himself who had saved my life when we were both five years old. The Methodist Church picnic was held at the State Park that year, right on the

18

Potomac River. A bunch of us were having a great time playing with big black inner tubes from Cody's dad's truck. We had them all tied together like a barge floating down the river. We were splashing in and out of the tubes, swimming through each other's legs, dunking and being dunked.

I was laying on top of the huge inner tube, feeling the sun's hot rays scorching me right through to my spine, when a stomach cramp shot out of nowhere, curling me right off the tube and back into the water. I went down and under like a river rock. Cody lunged at me, a big grin on his face 'cause he was going to dunk me one good. When he saw me dunking myself, he knew right off something was wrong. Cody remembered what our kindergarten teacher had said just a few days before about emergencies. Whenever you need an adult quick, she announced, open your mouth and yell, "Fire!" at the top of your lungs.

Cody climbed back on top of his inner tube and started hollering, "Fire! Fire!" so loud that ten or twenty mothers popped up off their towels and came a-running, half of them scared to death that the South Potomac was ablaze.

"Kitty Lee's drowning!" he shrieked as they got closer, all the while reaching under the water and grabbing onto my hair, my leg, anything he could find. He'd lift up a foot and then lose it, snatch an elbow or a knee and try to yank me up.

Pop and Gramma both laughed later, saying it was really Mrs. Wainwright who dove in and pulled all of me out. But if you listened to Cody Baines tell the story, Mrs. Wainwright just got in his way. Cody changes the story a little each time he tells it, adding or ignoring various facts.

Cody swears that when he saw me down under the water, he pulled me up and tossed me on top of his inner tube and paddled me to shore. But Cody changes his story as often as his socks. By the time we were in the third grade he told the whole playground that he tied me on the handlebars of his red tricycle and raced straight to the hospital.

"Hey, Cody, what are you doing out here this late at night without your momma?" I joked. I walked right up to him, glad to feel his heavy arm go around my shoulders.

Up close I was surprised to see how tall and broad Cody had grown in the past few months. He was as big as Pop. I could smell after shave. I craned my neck another inch and saw the dark shadows of his whiskers along his square jaw.

"Are you going to the movies, or do you have to go back and push more cones at Jake's?"

"Movies. Dottie can't come. She probably has to baby-sit Ludy."

Cody's two friends started to laugh.

"Yeah, I wonder how much she gets paid an hour," James hooted.

"Nobody in this town can afford her, that's for damn sure," snickered Monroe.

"What's that supposed to mean?" I wanted to know. Everybody in town knew Dottie's father up and left the whole family five years ago. Ever since then Dottie had to help out with expenses and take care of her little brother, Ludy. Dottie had

had a job in the dime store after school since she was thirteen.

Cody frowned at his friends and gave James a shove on the arm. "Go on. I'll catch up with you later."

"See you, Kitty," called out James. "If you ever get tired of making root beer floats, I'll be glad to let you baby-sit me."

Both boys laughed hard, shaking their heads.

"What are they talking about?" I crossed my arms and scowled at them both. "Honestly, Cody, your friends are sick. How can you associate with them, anyway?"

Cody grinned and tugged at my hair. "They don't mean anything, Kitty. We just saw Dottie a bit ago, that's all." Cody scratched his jaw and grinned. "And when we saw her, she wasn't baby-sitting Ludy, that's for sure."

I broke away and looked down the street, smiling. "Well, that's great then. Is she coming to the movies after all?"

Cody took my elbow as we crossed the street. "Well . . . I don't think so. Looked to me like Dottie was on some sort of a date up at the diner."

"What?" The warm summer air suddenly felt clammy on my bare arms. Dottie wouldn't go and get herself dated up without telling me every single detail the moment it happened. Dottie and I called each other at least three times a day, even if nothing new had happened.

I chewed on my lip, walking beside Cody. "It couldn't be a *real* date, Cody. I would have known all about it. I bet it's her cousin Lenny down from

Cumberland. Did he have red hair and real big feet?"

Cody snorted. "If it were her cousin, then they were definitely 'kissing cousins,' if you know what I mean."

I reached out and slapped Cody right on the arm. "Listen to you! You sound as bad as James and your other low-life friends. This is *Dottie* we're talking about."

Cody rubbed his arm and looked offended. "Hey, don't get mad at me, Kitty. I'm just telling you what I saw, is all. Dottie was practically sitting on this guy's lap, and she had her hand right on his arm the whole time he was trying to eat his sandwich."

"Well, who in the world is he then?"

Cody shook his head. "He's not from Romney, or the high school, that's for sure. I bet this guy is twenty-five if he's a day."

I stopped dead in my tracks. Dottie, on a real date? With a twenty-five-year-old man nobody in town even knew? I shivered then, spooked. Just when you think you know someone like a book, they go and add another chapter.

"Where do you think she met him?" I asked. Romney was small enough for a stranger to stick out like a sore thumb. "He's not *really* twenty-five, is he, Cody?"

Cody sighed. "Hey, I didn't interview the guy, Kitty Lee. But I think he's been hired with the lawn crew up at the shoe factory. A new man, a Mr. Curtis, bought the factory and now he's making all sorts of changes — adding a skylight, planting new grass and trees."

"So, did Dottie's date have his lawn mower with him or something?" It burned me a little that Cody had so many facts and I didn't have a one.

Cody laughed. "Yes, see, he rode his mower to the diner . . ." Cody rubbed his knuckles against my head. "He must work for some landscaper 'cause he was wearing a T-shirt with a rake stenciled on the back."

I groaned, wondering if Dottie cared if her new date wore such a shirt to the diner. It was Romney's best and only restaurant; some men even wore ties on Sundays.

"Come on, Kitty, Dottie looked happy to me. We'd better hurry because the movie's about to start. You can sit with me."

Cody treated me to a ticket and I followed his large shape down the darkened aisle. I still couldn't believe Dottie had a date. Maybe she just met this fellow today and that's why she came down to the Dairy Queen to tell me. If I hadn't been so busy, she would have told me all about him. Dottie would probably be sitting on my front porch when I got home from the movie, just bursting with news to share. Well, good for Dottie! Now she could start her senior year with lots of things to brag about. Jessica LaShay wasn't the only girl in town who could attract older men.

Cody yanked me down in my seat and handed me half his Milky Way. Cody and I used to share our candy bars when the two of us went to movies together Saturday afternoon. His momma would drop us off at eleven sharp, and we would walk back to Gramma Belle's for cookies and milk after. That gave us lots of time to talk about the movie and argue whether those movie stars really kissed each other or just pretended. I laughed, almost choking on my candy bar. Cody and I swore we would never, ever, trade spit with somebody by kissing them right on the mouth.

Cody elbowed me, pointing to the screen. "Hey, girl, I'm trying to watch a movie here."

I looked around the theater, checking who was with whom. Dottie would want to know everything she missed. I made some mental notes: 1) Jessica had her head on Allan Ruthers's shoulder. 2) James and his immature pals were in the back row, tossing popcorn and whistling. 3) Karen and her twin were already kissing the two seniors from West Ridge High. . . . I twisted around in my seat, staring back at James and his friends. If it weren't for James and his rude friends, Cody and I would still be coming to movies together. Even back in the seventh grade, we were still having a good time with each other. At last we were old enough to go to the evening show and walk home alone. Nothing else had changed. We still shared Milky Ways and talked the whole way home. Then one Saturday night Cody's friends sat right behind us. All through the show they kicked the backs of our seats and whispered, "Kiss her, Cody," or "Love birds, chirp, chirp" so bad that neither one of us could concentrate on the movie. And on the way back to Gramma Belle's we were both so embarrassed that we'd run out of things to say before we ever left Main Street. Somewhere in the middle of seventh grade, Cody stopped waiting for me outside the theater. That's when I started going to the Regent with Dottie.

Dottie! I let out a sigh so deep, Cody jumped. "You okay?" he whispered.

I nodded, not really understanding why I felt so bad. Maybe it was Dottie being at the diner with a stranger and me remembering how Cody stopped waiting for me out front. My eyes went back up to the screen, but I couldn't stop shivering. Either the Regent's air-conditioning was on the fritz again or life was confusing me.

Cody looked at me and then put his arm around the back of my chair, his huge warm fingers cupping my shoulder. I smiled at him, feeling better. Cody was such a nice guy. Studying his strong profile in the flickering light, I was struck with how handsome he had become. Cody was going to be the starting quarterback this year. It wouldn't surprise me at all if every girl in the senior class started scribbling his name all over their notebooks as soon as school started. Maybe Cody had a crush on one of the girls right now and was just too shy to do anything about it. I felt so proud of Cody then I could almost feel myself swell. I leaned over and tapped his chest. "Hey, Cody, how come you don't bring real girls to the movies?"

Cody smiled so wide his white teeth lit up his face. He tapped his finger on my nose. "What do you mean, a *real* girl? Are you plastic or something?"

"Course not," I laughed, leaning my head back against his arm and enjoying the feeling of the good old days again. "But I'm not your *date* either."

I could feel Cody's arm go rigid then, like he

had just turned to stone. Then he took his arm away so fast my head banged against the back of the seat.

"What's wrong, Cody?" I asked, rubbing my head.

Cody just glared at me for a full minute before he turned back to the screen, staring at it like his life depended on memorizing the actor's lines.

I chewed the rest of the Milky Way, taking peeks at Cody every now and then. His jaw, his chest, and even both legs were rigid now.

I didn't know what I had said. At first I thought he was mad 'cause I was minding his business. I wasn't trying to tease him. In the past few years Cody had brought lots of girls to the movies. Dottie and I would giggle about each one of them. But they weren't real girls. I mean, half of them were cousins and the rest were the kind who just hung around the lobby waiting for some boy to ask them to sit with him.

None of them were real *call-up-ahead-of-time* girls.

I rolled my wrapper up in a tiny ball and sighed again. This time Cody didn't even look at me. In fact, he leaned so far to the left in his seat no part of him was touching me. Gramma Belle said all teenagers should come with their own set of directions and I was beginning to believe her.

I was watching the movie, wondering where exactly Dottie could have met this lawn man, when something hit me on the back of the neck. Right off I thought it was Cody, pinching me. But then something else bounced off my neck. Shoot, if James or Monroe wanted a fight, they sure

26

picked the right night. I was so mad I would knock them all down a rat hole.

I twisted around, looking for someone to clobber. As soon as I did, another ping stung me. I heard giggling from several rows behind me to the left. I squinted in the dim light, studying each row of seats. I stopped midcenter and stared at the white Mercedes family. The father sat calmly, his hands holding a large tub of popcorn. He was staring straight ahead at the flickering screen, while his three kids were busy pelting half of Romney with Good & Plenty.

I caught the eye of the little boy. He caught mine and stared right back at me for a second. Then he reached in his candy box, pulled out a Good & Plenty, licked it quick, and threw it right in my face.

I was out of my seat in a second, knocking over two or three tubs of popcorn as I scooted down the aisle toward the little boy.

"Why are you throwing candy at me?" I asked, grabbing the box of Good & Plenty from his hand.

"Daddy!" shrieked the little boy. "That girl stole my candy!"

I could hear a tin reel drop in the projection room. A few people in the back told me to go sit down, and Monroe started to chant, "Fight, fight, fight!"

"Leave the kid alone," mumbled someone in front. It sounded like Cody.

I bent down and pulled on the Mercedes man's sleeve. "Mister, your son has been hitting me with candy . . ."

The man looked up at me, then back down at

his son. "But Joey has been sitting here with me."

Joey screwed up his face and frowned at me.

"Hey, I'm not making this up. I was just trying to watch a movie, mister."

"Pick on someone your own size, Kitty!" James called out.

Lots of people started to laugh. I didn't even smile. Things were piling up so fast inside of me I felt like I was being crowded out of myself. Glory Ned, anyway! I cringed, hearing how much I sounded like Gramma Belle. First Dottie sneaking around with some total stranger, then Cody growing up overnight and getting mad at me for no good reason, and now a passel of strangers following me around Romney making my life miserable and pelting me with Good & Plenty.

I thrust the little boy's candy at his father and stomped up the aisle. I was outside, trying to slow down my heart, when the double doors clanged open. Out came the tall Mercedes man, carrying the littlest girl and pushing his son ahead of him with impatient shoves. Janice was following behind, tears rolling down her cheeks, and both hands covering her ears.

"Stop it," Joey snapped.

"Go on, Joey. Apologize to the young lady. You're eight years old and still acting like a baby."

"I'm not a baby!" Joey glared at his father, then me. He shoved both hands deep into the pockets of his shorts and stared at the sidewalk. Finally he drew in a deep breath. "I'm sorry I hit you with my candy," he said quickly. He waited a second before he added, "But you were mean to take my candy. You're mean and I don't like you."

28

"Joey!" His father bent down and gave Joey's arm a shake.

"Don't fight!" cried Chrissy, hiding her face against her father's chest.

"Hey," I said quickly. "Apology accepted. It's okay, no harm done." I tried to smile wide enough for all of them. "I was . . . well, I guess I got a little too upset, myself. It's been a bad day."

The Mercedes man looked at me then, our eyes locking for a long minute. He looked glad that I was having a bad day, too. Like we had something in common.

I knelt down on one knee and smiled at Joey. "Tell you what. If you come to the movies next Saturday, I'll be sure and buy you a new box of candy, okay?"

Joey nodded. "Promise?"

"Sure, if you promise not to toss any at the audience. Is it a deal?" I stuck out my hand. A light flickered briefly in Joey's eyes, but he shoved his hands in his pockets instead.

"Make sure it's a big box," he mumbled softly.

The Mercedes man reached out and shook my hand, drawing me up to stand beside him. "Excuse his bad manners." He gave my hand a firm shake and let it drop. "I remember you from the Dairy Queen. And I'm sure you're remembering the bad impressions we keep creating."

I shrugged, not sure if denying the truth would make things more awkward.

The man took Janice's hand and gave Chrissy a quick kiss on the cheek. "Well, we better head home and get ready for bed."

"We have to finish playing Candyland, Dad," reminded Joey. "You promised."

The man smiled at his son. "Okay. We better hurry then." He turned to me. "You go back inside and enjoy the rest of the movie with your date."

"Oh, Cody isn't my date," I said quickly. "Just a friend."

The man grinned. Up close he looked almost Cody's age. As he brushed past me, my heart tripped like it was stumbling down some stairs. This man was so good-looking it embarrassed me. I couldn't stop staring at his mouth, his eyes, his hair . . .

"I almost forgot." The man turned back to me. "My name is Brad Curtis and this is my son, Joey. These are my daughters, Chrissy and Janice."

"I'm Kitty Lee Carter."

"Well, Kitty Lee Carter, the next time you see us, I'm sure it will be under happier circumstances."

I watched as Mr. Curtis herded his children down the sidewalk, glad when he set Chrissy down and gave Joey a quick hug. He did like his kids, that was for sure.

I crossed the street and walked to the diner. As I pressed my face up close I could see that all of the stools and most of the booths were empty. Cody's mom was busy at the counter, filling up napkin dispensers. The other waitress had her shoes off and her feet up, smoking a cigarette and relaxing till the movie broke up and the crowd came in for a late-night piece of pie and coffee.

All of a sudden I felt a flicker of guilt, thinking about Cody sitting all by himself at the Regent.

The guilt only lasted a second, washed out quick by remembering how he didn't even come outside to check on me when I stormed out. He was too busy acting like a macho man.

I scanned the diner one last time. Dottie and her mystery man weren't inside at all.

Thinking back, I should have come to the diner right away, before the movie even started. I should have raced up to Dottie, grabbing her by the arm and dragging her right out of there. I should have forced her to leave with me, before she stayed and *left* with him. It might have made some sort of difference.

Chapter Four

"What's wrong with you this morning, Kitty Lee? You've been sitting here twenty minutes and you haven't even touched your breakfast." Gramma Belle pushed my cereal bowl an inch closer. "You can't expect to work a full day at Jake's and then sit up half the night watching a movie and drag in here too tired to . . ."

"I was home by nine-thirty. Anyway, it's too hot to eat." I sipped my juice.

Gramma snatched up the cereal bowl, making a big production of pouring the milk and untouched cornflakes down the drain. She clanged the spoon around the bottom of the bowl like she was ringing home the cows.

"Waste not, want not . . ." grumbled Gramma. She whipped the dish towel off the hook with a loud snap.

"Is Pop up yet?"

Gramma shook her head. "No, your father is *not* up yet. He has three jobs lined up and no telling how long his customers are going to wait for their roofs to be patched and their decks to be tacked on. Wouldn't surprise me if all three jobs ended up at Gaston's Construction." Gramma took a long sip of her coffee. "I swear, Kitty. That son of mine lays in that bed a few minutes later every day. Each time I peek inside, he closes his eyes and pretends to be asleep. Glory Ned, a grown man shouldn't start hiding his head in the sand like one of them ostriches." Gramma Belle leaned against the counter and rubbed her back. "I'm getting too old to be taking care of everybody. Who's going to take care of me is what I want to know."

Gramma's whole body shook as she went back to drying the bowl. Her mouth was pulled down and she hadn't even put her teeth in yet. That was a bad sign, a real indicator that she was already knee-deep in the middle of a bad spell.

"I know it's hard on your pa every June. Lord, it's been fourteen years and he's all of a sudden acting like your momma just died last Tuesday."

Gramma put the dish away and let the cabinet door bang shut.

My mouth fell open. I wasn't used to Pop or Gramma Belle talking about my momma. I was too young to have any memories. Pop and Gramma Belle said she died in a car crash out on Highway 28 near the new mall that had just gone up. It had been raining and a truck ran a light. The police called Pop from the hospital and Pop called his own momma right away. Gramma caught the eleven-twenty out of Cumberland and she's been here ever since.

"And don't ask me who's going to fix our porch," said Gramma, refilling her cup and sinking down into the chair. "I'm ashamed to ask any of my friends to come over, not knowing which one is going to fall through that rotten board and have to be pulled out with a rope."

I swallowed anything I was thinking of saying back, like, "The board only creaks, Gramma, nobody is in any danger." Anything would be kindling to her morning fire. Besides, maybe if I kept quiet a little longer, she might start talking about Momma again. There was something nobody was telling me about that accident. Something shameful probably; that's why no one mentions it to me.

I finished my juice and rinsed and dried my glass. I knew I couldn't ask any questions this morning. Gramma's dark moods came and went, most of them only lasting for an hour or two, short and powerful as a summer storm. But I still hold my breath till they blow over. I wish I could just pull out a chair and make Gramma tell me everything she knew about Momma. Not only how she died, but how she lived. Over the years I've gathered bits and pieces of talk. Sometimes listening to Gramma and her friends as they sat on the front porch or late at night when Pop and Gramma thought I was asleep. Once when I was playing out back in Cody's yard, his mom and her friends said, "Too bad about Kitty's momma. Maybe the day she got in that car she was having one of her bad days."

34

Momma looked so young and pretty in all of her pictures, much too lovely to have *bad days*.

I turned and smiled at Gramma. Her bad days could disappear real fast if she felt like gossiping. "Hey, Gramma . . . I met a new family in town last night. His name is Mr. Curtis, the man who bought the shoe factory from the Wilsons. He drives a white Mercedes Benz and has three little kids."

Gramma shifted in her seat and grunted, tapping fingers on the table. She wasn't ready to give up her bad mood so quick.

"Oh, Gramma, he is the most handsome man I have ever seen. His hair is blond, almost white, the way Cody's used to be, and he has these blue eyes that are real, cool blue. Like he can see right into the center of a person."

Gramma grunted. "Let's just hope he doesn't lay off half the town. You have to wonder why a stranger would bring all his money into a small town like Romney."

I laughed at Gramma. I knew once she met Mr. Curtis she would probably ask him over for some iced tea. "Cody says he's adding lots of nice touches to the factory. Maybe we can go up and see it sometime."

Gramma stretched out both feet, still wrapped in her knitted brown slippers. "I wonder if I'll be walking at all in a couple of months. My ankles are swelling up like water balloons already. Wouldn't surprise me if I had some sort of sugar problem."

I bit down on my lip so I wouldn't smile. I know Gramma Belle wanted me to ask her why she thought that. But I didn't. When a body is digging themselves into a foul mood, questions are just like handing them a shovel.

"Mr. Curtis sure doesn't look like the daddy of three, that's for sure." I peeked over at Gramma. She twisted in her chair and rubbed her back. "He looks so young."

"I can't rightly remember being young," she said finally. She jerked her thumb toward Pop's closed bedroom door. "Your father isn't even forty and he acts older than I do. I told him last Sunday to go down and talk to Reverend Peters if he was having a hard time with things. He got so mad he took off his tie and wouldn't even go to services with me. Your pop has himself a real problem, all right."

I glanced at the closed door. I agreed with Gramma. Pop was acting so distant lately. Yesterday he sat in his chair with the newspaper in his lap for an hour and didn't even turn a page.

Gramma pushed her coffee cup away and lay her head down on the gray Formica top like she was about to expire.

"Are you okay, Gramma?" I asked.

The kitchen clock ticked loudly. Gramma's soft rounded back heaved up and down.

"I'm just wore out," she said.

I leaned against the kitchen counter, my pop with his closed door and Gramma laying on the table like her spine had dissolved. The last two remaining members of my family and they both were acting like life wasn't worth waking up for.

"Mr. Curtis seems nice, but his wife sure has a problem." I said it slowly and then waited to see

36

if Gramma was going to take my bait. It was hard not to smile, watching Gramma trying to decide if she should take on some fresh gossip.

"How so?" she finally asked.

I walked a little closer. "Sorry, Gramma, I can't hear you."

Gramma's head shot up and she glared at me like she knew darn well I could hear her. "Why do you think Mrs. Curtis has a problem?"

I hopped up on the counter and swung my legs back and forth. "Well, the first time I saw her was at the Dairy Queen when she stuck her head out the window and hollered at Mr. Curtis and the kids to hurry up. Then last night her little girl fell and skinned her knees and Mrs. Curtis yelled some more. She fussed at the little girl and walked off in a huff."

"Anything else?" Gramma looked slightly disappointed.

"Well, I call that quite a bit for one day, wouldn't you?"

Gramma heaved herself up off the chair and sighed. "If I were you, I wouldn't be telling people that Mrs. Curtis has a problem. Sounds to me like all she has is a temper."

I was so shocked I nearly fell in the sink. "A temper *is* a problem."

Gramma just grunted and unlatched the screen door to let the cat in. "No, a *problem* is what your pop is liable to have unless he gets out of that bed and back on his feet. Comes a time when you've got to get over personal tragedies and keep on living."

I knew the personal tragedy she was talking

about was my momma's accident. "Pop still misses her a lot."

Gramma nodded. "That fool truck ran the light and killed your momma." When Gramma looked over and saw my sad face, she gave me a sorry smile like she knew she had clung onto her bad mood too long. "Now, I'm going outside to check the garden. Be sure and don't ask your pop any questions about the accident. He's liable to go to bed for a month of Sundays."

The screen door slammed shut. Any mention of my momma seemed to take the sail right out of everybody.

Working in the garden would be fine for Gramma. By lunchtime she would be laughing about the size of her cucumbers and radishes. As I walked past Pop's door I pounded on it with my balled-up fist. "Rise and shine," I called out. "You up in there, Pop?"

It was still dead quiet so I pounded again. I heard Pop coughing and the bed squeaking. "I'm up," he called back.

I opened the door and grinned in. Pop rubbed his eyes with one hand and gave a small salute with the other.

"Morning, kitten," he said and yawned.

"Morning, Pop. Coffee's made and Gramma's biscuits are getting cold."

As I closed the door, the phone started to ring. I raced back into the kitchen and grabbed the phone on the fourth ring. "Hello?"

"Kitty, hi. It's me, Dottie."

I hopped back up on the counter and leaned

against the wall. "Well, I was just about to call you. Tell me all about last night."

Dottie was quiet on the other end of the phone for a long minute. Finally she spoke. "What do you mean?"

I laughed, wondering if Dottie had some sort of joke going with Cody, both of them trying to keep the facts from me. "I mean, what did you *do* last night?"

Dottie waited another beat. "Oh, gosh, nothing much. Momma went out and I had to watch Ludy again. I sat around, watching television and eating too much popcorn. Same old stuff."

I pulled the phone from my ear and frowned. Was Dottie teasing me?

"Dottie, come on, what did you really do last night?"

The other end was silent, letting me know my best friend was lying to me through her teeth.

Chapter Five

"Dottie, you know darn well you weren't baby-sitting Ludy last night." I couldn't believe what I was hearing. Since when did Dottie start lying, especially to me? "Are you going to tell me who you were with at the diner or do I have to wait and hear it from Cody and his lunatic friends?" I didn't care if I was being rude; best friends shouldn't keep secrets.

Dottie groaned on the other end. "Boy, I forgot how hard it was to try and keep something from you. You're a regular bloodhound."

I didn't laugh. What was funny about Dottie trying her hardest to keep something from me? Wasn't I the one who walked down with her to Woolworth's to get her first bra in the sixth grade and didn't she call me up at eleven-thirty to tell me that Jason Klemmer finally got up his nerve to kiss her good night after the Christmas dance two years ago?

"So who is he, Dottie? And why are you so ashamed of him that he's a secret?"

"I'm not a bit ashamed of him, Kitty. I've just been so busy and . . ." Dottie giggled. "He is so cute. His name is Ronnie O'Brien. He's doing some land sculpturing over at the shoe factory."

"Land sculpturing? You mean he's helping them put in a new hedge?"

"Well, it's a lot more involved than *that*, Kitty Lee," Dottie snapped. Her voice had fur standing straight up.

"Well, how am I supposed to know how involved it is when you've been keeping him a secret? Listen, Dottie. I have to get ready for work now. Can you bring this Ronnie character down to the Dairy Queen tomorrow? I'll treat you both to a root beer. I can hardly wait to meet him, honest."

"Well . . ." Dottie paused. She was probably chewing on the end of her hair, same as she always did when she was stalling. "Ronnie is really busy sculpting. He's even working today as a favor to Mr. Curtis. Ronnie said that three more truck-loads of trees are coming in from Fort Ashby tomorrow, and they have to be in the ground before the sun gets too hot. He'll be busy for the next two days at least."

"Well, how about when he gets off work?"

"I just can't say, Kitty. Ronnie likes to unwind after he sculpts."

Fast as could be, I smacked my hand over my mouth to keep the laugh in. Dottie was talking about this Ronnie like he was some sort of Michelangelo. Gramma Belle is forever telling me to keep my sense of humor where it belongs. "It's easier for a rich man to ride through God's gates than for some smart mouth who doesn't know when to keep his mouth shut."

I hung up, not quite sure if I was ever going to meet Dottie's new boyfriend. I could understand her not wanting to introduce Ronnie to a flirt like Jessica, but I was her best friend. Maybe Ronnie got tongue-tied around new people. Maybe Dottie was trying to relax him before they went public about liking each other.

After I showered, I tied my thick damp hair up in a ponytail. I scowled at my reflection, counting another five or six freckles laying across my nose. I was starting to look more like six than sixteen. I took my toothbrush and combed my heavy dark eyebrows up. Maybe I should take a bus into Cumberland and have them waxed. My friend Charlene Foster got a gift certificate from an aunt and waxed off just about everything that was offered at Wendy's Wax-a-Rama. Now her eyebrows were edged as sharp as rooftops. I grinned again, thinking of Ronnie bragging to Dottie about being an artist with a rake. And Dottie swallowing it all up and bragging back for him.

I jumped into my uniform and gave Pop and Gramma a kiss good-bye. They were both in the garden and everyone seemed pretty happy with the day.

At the intersection of Maple and Main I could see Cody and his smart-aleck friends talking, so I turned and walked an extra five blocks just so I wouldn't have to walk past them. Cody would probably just ignore me or laugh when James made some crack about Dottie and her lawn mower man. I was so late by the time I hit Chestnut Street, I started to run. Jake trusted me to be at my window at exactly ten o'clock sharp. Lots of people headed down after the nine o'clock service let out. By the time I hit the parking lot, I had a side stitch. I couldn't even slow down since there were already three people backed up outside my window. I hurried across the lot. All of a sudden, I felt dizzy; white dots dancing in front of my eyes.

I tried to walk through the dots, rubbing my hands over my cold and prickly arms. I was just light-headed since I had skipped breakfast. I thought I'd feel better once I got inside Jake's. But as I headed across the parking lot, ten little Dairy Queens circled around me like ring around the rosy.

I put my hands over my face for a second, then looked briefly into the worried blue eyes of Mr. Bradley Curtis before I fainted dead away.

Chapter Six

The smooth leather of Mr. Curtis's car seat smelled good, like the old baseball glove Pop used to oil for me. I smiled.

"She's smiling, Dad!" shouted someone.

"She isn't a bit dead," added another high voice. It sounded disappointed.

When I opened my eyes, I was slumped in the front seat of the Mercedes, while Mr. Curtis and his three little kids surrounded me like a fence.

Mr. Curtis helped me sit up. "Are you all right?"

"Yeah," I said, rubbing my head. "I think so."

"You fainted and my daddy caught you," announced Janice.

"And don't throw up in our car either," added Joey.

I put my hand on the handle. "I feel fine, now. Thanks."

Mr. Curtis pushed me gently back against the seat. "Sit here in the air-conditioned car for a while. It's already ninety degrees out there. Jake said I can drive you home if you want."

I opened the car door and smiled. I could see Jake was already plenty busy at the window. He would need all the help he could get today with the heat wave. Everyone would be wanting a cone before evening.

"I bet you don't have a car *this* nice," said Joey.

Quick as could be, Mr. Curtis whirled around and slapped Joey on the leg. "That's enough from you, young man."

Janice covered both eyes with her hands and Chrissy started crying, pushing herself back against the seat. But Joey didn't cry at all. He just stared right back at his daddy like he didn't like him at all.

Mr. Curtis twisted around and rubbed Joey's leg. "Sorry, son. I didn't mean to . . ."

But Joey just turned his head and stared out the window.

I felt bad for the little boy, the way he kept blinking fast so the tears wouldn't fall.

"Thank you for helping me," I said cheerfully. "You have a fun day, okay? Don't get too much of this good sunshine, though." When Joey glanced over at me, I leaned toward him. "There's lots of tadpoles in the creek behind the Dairy Queen. Maybe you can get a jar and catch some."

Joey opened his mouth to ask a question, but twisted away from me instead. "I hate tadpoles," he mumbled.

After I thanked everyone again, I hopped out of the car. Something was troubling that family; something was wrong.

I felt Mr. Curtis's hand on my shoulder as I reached for Jake's screen door. "Kitty, I want to apologize for my son."

"Oh, Joey didn't mean anything. Everyone gets a little cranky when it's hot like this." I glanced over at the car, knowing those little kids would much rather be in a swimming pool right now.

Inside I could hear Jake rattling his pots, clearing his throat, and slamming the freezer door shut; Jake's subtle way of telling me that if I could stand, he sure could use me inside.

Mr. Curtis reached out and took my elbow, pulling me back from the screen door. "My family hasn't been in Romney very long, Kitty Lee. I was wondering if you could help me out with the kids for a few weeks?"

"Isn't your wife still here?"

Mr. Curtis looked startled at first. "Sure. She's here. But, she isn't feeling all that well and . . ." Mr. Curtis kept sticking his hands in and out of his pockets. "We sure could use your help."

Jake opened the screen door and stuck his head out. "You ready to come in, Kitty? You feeling okay, now?"

I nodded, knowing that Jake wanted me inside quick. He flicked his cigarette out and let the door slam hard behind him.

"I wish I could help you, Mr. Curtis, but I already have a job here with Jake." I'd nodded my head toward the screen door. "In fact, I'd better get inside right now."

Mr. Curtis caught hold of my arm again. "You're good with my kids." Mr. Curtis glanced through the screen door at Jake and lowered his voice. "I don't know what you're making here, but I'll pay you three times more an hour."

I grinned. That was a good offer, all right. Three times what I was making at Jake's would put the keys to my new car in my hand a whole lot faster. But the clattering of pans inside brought me back to Jake's. Jake was counting on me for the whole summer. "Sounds good, but I already promised Jake I would work all summer. I'll be glad to ask around for you, Mr. Curtis."

He shook his head. "I want you." He ran his hand through his hair and sighed. "Listen, I'll talk to Jake for you." Mr. Curtis laughed. "Hell, I'll work the window for you if you would help me out with the children."

I grinned. "No, don't do that, Mr. Curtis. I really do think I should stay here and help Jake."

I opened the door, then stopped to watch Mr. Curtis walk slowly to his car. From the back he looked just like any high school kid. You couldn't tell from looking that he was weighed down with such a big family. As Mr. Curtis slid behind the wheel he turned and looked right at me. He just nodded, like he knew I'd be watching him. I let the screen door slam shut, my whole face burning up again. The way my heart was beating should have warned me to stay right where I was and let Mr. Curtis figure out his own problems. Why did I go and get red-faced every time I talked to him?

"We need a double order of fries, Kitty Lee," called out Jake. "Get a fresh bag from the freezer!"

I jumped, knocking a can of opened kidney beans off the counter. As I bent down to scoop up the beans, I started to worry. What if Mr. Curtis came back, asking me again to come and help him out? The thought of earning all that extra money was tempting. I could probably even get an AM/FM radio in my car if I took him up on his offer.

"I need those fries, sweetheart!" hollered Jake.

I stood up quick and hurried over to the freezer. Those Curtis kids needed a summer, I needed a car, and it sure wasn't every day that someone offered me that kind of money.

I grabbed the ten-pound bag of fries from the freezer and shivered. Maybe I was shaking hard from the freezer, or maybe it was because I knew, even then, that I was tempted by Mr. Curtis's offer.

Chapter Seven

I had the next two days off, but I was so bored I almost called Jake to ask him if I couldn't come back early. Every time I called Dottie she was on her way out the door. She sounded so happy, so glad to be so busy with her new boyfriend. Even though I was happy for her, I felt unhappy knowing she didn't have any time for me. Gramma Belle and her friends were busy organizing the annual Methodist Flea Market Extravaganza, and Pop insisted he pulled his back out and closed his bedroom door earlier than ever each day.

On Tuesday I walked up to town. I saw Cody and James coming out of the drugstore.

"Hey, good-looking!" James hollered from the other side of the street. "I almost didn't recognize you without your little uniform."

I just nodded at James, my eyes glued to the back of Cody's head. If he just turned around once, I would smile at him and let him know that

49

I wasn't mad about anything. But he got into his car and slammed the door. I ran into the first store I came to, not wanting him to think I didn't have anything to do with my summer.

Fact was, with Dottie so tied up with her new boyfriend, and most of my other friends on vacation, I *didn't* have anything much to do. Working at Jake's was the perfect place for me. Jake was so busy he said he could use me almost every day.

"I'm willing to work any shift," I'd promised him. From the way my summer was starting off, I wouldn't be doing anything else. Jake had laughed at the time, but he took me up on my offer. By Saturday afternoon at four o'clock, I felt as if I had been on my feet for a hundred hours straight. On the way home, all I could think about was getting into a hot tub.

"Hey there, lady!" Dottie called out. She was sitting on my porch swing waiting for me. I took the steps two at a time and gave her a hug. I felt wonderful. It had been such a long time since she had just dropped by.

"Hi, stranger," we both said at the same time, laughing. I raced inside and slipped into my shorts so we could walk down to Stoney Creek Park and back. I was humming as I slipped into my tennis shoes, forgetting about my blisters since I was so happy to have my best friend back on my front porch.

"Okay now, Dottie, since you are intent on hiding your boyfriend, tell me at least two things about him. Is he cute? Does he have his own car? Hey, where did he go to high school, anyway?"

"That's three questions, Kitty," Dottie pointed out. "Yes, he's very cute, least ways *I* think so. Yes, he has his own car. He calls it the Red Baron and it's real old but at least it still runs. And he graduated high school in Pinto two years ago." Dottie pulled off a handful of leaves as we rounded the corner. "Or maybe it was three years, I forget." Dottie laughed. "Gosh, Kitty, Ronnie and I have been together for hours and hours, talking non-stop about everything in the world, and I still don't know everything about him."

Dottie let the leaves fall from her hands and smiled so serenely she looked almost holy. "He is so nice, Kitty. I can't wait for you to meet him. We can talk for hours and never run dry. He thinks I am the smartest girl he's ever met."

"You *are* smart." Dottie could probably swing a scholarship if she really buckled down this year.

"I'm not smart. I just read a lot, is all. Ronnie likes to read, too. His favorite poet is e. e. cummings. Isn't that great? I mean, I can't think of one boy in our class who even *has* a favorite poet."

Right off I thought of Cody and how much he liked Robert Frost, especially the poem about stopping by the woods on a snowy night. Cody told me once that he felt that way about driving past his granddaddy's farm the first Christmas after it had been sold. Cody said that he wanted to just stand there forever, pretending that the lights shining from the farmhouse were his grand-daddy's.

Dottie didn't know about *all* of the men in Romney. She hadn't even met Mr. Curtis yet. You could tell by just looking at Mr. Curtis that he was smart. He probably had a whole leather-bound collection of poetry in his big house on the hill. Our English teacher at the high school had read us lots of wonderful poems this year. I smiled, imagining Mr. Curtis's face leaning toward me, reciting Christopher Marlowe . . . "Whoever loved that loved not at first sight?" I sighed. Love at first sight had to be the most passionate of all.

Dottie tugged on my ponytail. "Hey, you listening to me?"

I nodded, biting my lip and blinking away the picture of Mr. Curtis standing next to the blazing fire, a book of poetry in one hand and the other stretched out to me. . . .

Dottie put her hand against my cheek. "You feeling all right? Maybe we better turn around and go get a soda, Kitty. Your face is as red as can be."

"I'm fine."

Dottie shook back her hair and grinned. "Okay, now where was I? Oh, yeah, last night Ronnie said he might go back to finish up his last year at this junior college in Pittsburgh, or maybe he will start his own sculpting business near Harrisburg. Course, if he does that he'll need at least five or six thousand dollars to buy equipment."

I let one eyebrow shoot up, but managed to bring it down fast before Dottie could see. I had to meet this Ronnie fast to make sure he wasn't some sort of fruitcake. Dottie and her mom didn't have any money, and you could tell that as soon as you pulled into their gravel drive. Ever since Dottie's dad left, the house has been getting more and more worn-out looking. Ronnie wouldn't be thinking that he could ask Dottie to invest in his sculpting business.

"Being with Ronnie has really made me feel feminine, more womanly. He walks on the outside of the sidewalk, opens my car door without me asking. I swear Kitty Lee, can you imagine Cody or his friends ever acting that way? Those boys still think it's funny to shove us in the hedges when we're all dressed up to go to a dance."

"I know." I couldn't help but grin, remembering when Cody slid a tadpole down the front of Mary Louise Duggan's dress the year she was so proud of being the first to have real cleavage. "I guess it's because we all grew up in each other's backyards."

"Maybe," Dottie said with a frown. "They are such *boys* compared to Ronnie. I just hope you meet someone like my Ronnie one day so you can realize how wonderful it is to feel like a woman."

I stopped short. Feel like a woman? Shoot, I was still trying to get the hang of feeling like a teenager.

"It makes you feel like a woman when he opens your car door?" I huffed. I started walking a little faster, not sure if I even wanted an answer. I had read enough books myself, including some shockers that Dottie's cousin had left last summer, to know exactly what kind of carrying on makes you suddenly feel like a woman.

"Dottie Ramsey, I hope you aren't thinking about doing something stupid and dangerous with this boy, are you?" I was just about to remind Dottie about Loretta Alberts, only seventeen, who had a baby last year and was working two jobs

53

just to help her husband pay the rent.

"Of course not. There's a whole lot more to our relationship than just the physical. Just forget it, okay?" she said, closing me out like I couldn't possibly understand.

Dottie must have been watching my face and saw how hurt I looked, so she took another stab at it.

"All I meant, Kitty, is I feel more like a woman because Ronnie is older and treats me so grown-up. He listens to what I'm saying. He's not like my mother, always finishing a sentence for me and then telling me how I should be feeling about things. Ronnie will be twenty-one at the end of August. He's just so much more intense about things 'cause he already knows what he wants out of life. He makes me feel like I better start knowing what I want out of life, too."

Dottie's voice grew soft, her eyes lighting up in an odd way. Like there was some sort of dimmer deep inside her just now turning on.

I kept quiet for a while, knowing that I didn't really understand how Dottie felt right now. It made me feel kind of left out. Up until then we had usually shared just about the same kind of feelings. Even when her dad left in the middle of the night, I understood. It was kind of like my momma dying before I even knew who she was. Now an older man was giving her new feelings. Last Christmas I went out with a college freshman, Mary Lou's cousin visiting from Fort Lauderdale. He didn't light up anything inside me. I spent half the night listening to him tell me about his great football plays and the other half reminding him that we were not on the football field now and to please stop trying to tackle me. And, I talked with Mr. Curtis. I had talked to *lots* of older men and I felt like me the whole time.

We walked for another quarter mile, just thinking. I was trying hard to remember to mind my own business. Course I kept reminding myself that Dottie was my best friend in the whole world, which made her my business.

"Just remember, Dottie," I finally said. "Ronnie will be leaving at the end of the summer so don't go doing something stupid."

Dottie swung around so fast, her face so full of pain, I gasped. "I love him, Kitty Lee. I love him so much I can hardly wait till I'm with him again. Sometimes I just walk past the shoe factory so I can see him, so I can make sure that I haven't been dreaming up this whole time together."

She buried her face in her hands then and just cried hard. Cried as hard as we both did when we were back in the seventh grade, sitting side by side at the Regent, watching *Gone With the Wind* and knowing Scarlett was messing up her life for good by lying to Rhett. But this time I was making Dottie cry. I felt so guilty. "Hey now, Dottie," I said, putting my arm around her. "If you're so much in love, why are you crying? People driving past are going to think you're nuts, crying along Highway Twenty-eight." I hummed a few bars of a country song we both knew and then started singing as loud as I could. "Crying over Ronnie 'cause he's late for a date, crying over Ronnie on High-way Twenty-eight!"

Dottie looked up and started laughing, wiping

her tears with the back of both hands. "Oh, be quiet." Then she reached out and hugged me real tight and long like she was ready to board a plane and fly right out of my life.

Dottie had only known Ronnie for a few weeks, and she already thought she loved him. I knew all about spontaneous combustion from school, but outside of romantic poetry in books, I had never heard about spontaneous love before.

"You sure must love him a lot, Dottie."

"I do," said Dottie in a voice so quiet and sincere, it sounded like an amen.

I knew then, as we turned around by the turnpike sign and headed back, that the only thing for me to do was to be happy for her. A true best friend can't start right in telling a person not to love someone when they want to so bad.

Maybe Dottie was just caught up in the glamour of love. Once September came, Ronnie would leave, school would start, and Ronnie would head back to Pittsburgh. Then maybe Dottie would slide back into feeling the way she did before she met Ronnie.

"Well, Dottie, I have to pick up some things at the store for Gramma Belle. Someone told her you don't have to boil the lasagna noodles anymore and she has to try it for herself!" I laughed, remembering how mad Gramma had been when she heard that, like people had deliberately been wasting her time all these years. "Want to come for dinner?"

Dottie shook her head. "No thanks. But . . . Kitty, can I ask a favor?" Dottie didn't even wait for an answer. "Ronnie wants me to go to a party in Fort Ashby this Saturday. It'll be a real late party, one of his friends is getting married. My mother doesn't want me to go." Dottie stopped and looked like she was going to start crying all over again. "In fact, my mother doesn't want me to see Ronnie anymore. She says it's because he's older, but I think it's really because she's mad he doesn't rant and rave about how beautiful she is like all the other boys do."

I nodded. Dottie's mother did look more like a sister than a mother, that was a fact. Especially since Dottie's dad left, and Mrs. Ramsey had dyed her hair red and lost twenty-four pounds.

"So I was wondering if I could tell my mother I was spending the night at your house on Saturday? I'll be getting in around midnight. You could just leave the back screen unlatched and I'll be real quiet."

"But . . . but, won't your mom see Ronnie pick you up?"

Dottie smiled like she had orchestrated the whole night already. "No. I'm going to meet him in the school playground at six. I told my mom I was going to go over to help Judy with her perm."

I dug into the gravel with my toe, shocked that a person who never told a lie in her whole life was now suddenly scattering them out like corn to the chicks.

"What am I going to tell Gramma Belle?"

"Tell her I had a special date. Leave the back screen unlatched and I'll be real quiet." Dottie looked straight into my eyes. "Thanks, I really do appreciate this, Kitty. I know you hate lying as much as I do, but . . . but my mother just hates

Ronnie for no good reason. She can't stand to see me this happy, I bet."

Dottie started to walk away. She stopped and turned back. "I owe you one, okay?"

I shook my head. Thinking back, I should have had her put that promise in writing.

"You're darn right, Dottie," I should have called back. "You owe me all right, and when I come knocking to collect, I want it without a lick of a fight."

But even then, it was too late.

Chapter Eight

Cody and his friends came down to the Dairy Queen the next afternoon. They didn't come up to the window right away to order; instead they sat on the picnic tables, laughing loud and flirting with every girl in town, even the loud twelve-year-old Anderson twins who had been wearing lipstick and eyeliner since they were ten.

Cody looked nice in his white-and-red-striped shirt and white shorts. It didn't surprise me at all when Jessica LaShay came right over to him like the other boys weren't even standing there. Cody had had a crush on her in the ninth grade. Back then, Cody and I had searched for one hour in Randle's Drugstore to pick out a Valentine card special enough for Jessica. My heart broke as much as his when she'd barely glanced at it, thanking Cody like he had just handed her a homework assignment. She had had so many others to open that year.

When Cody finally got off the bench and walked to the window, it was to order a Coke for Jessica.

"You need two straws with that?" I asked icily.

Cody grinned. "No, miss. I think we'll just share this one, thank you."

I bent the straw I was left holding in my hand, hoping Cody knew I was pretending it was his neck. He knew I didn't care for Jessica. And she must have remembered how much I used to care for Cody, because she was outdoing herself, running her fingers through his thick blond hair and marvelling at how strong and big he was. If Mrs. Bodnar hadn't been waiting in line for her float, I would have slammed the window on the two of them. Jessica was acting like some sort of pediatrician conducting an exam in the middle of Jake's parking lot.

Jake came early so I could leave at four. Cody and his friends were still there, laughing so loud and carrying on so much that I knew no-good James had probably snuck some beer down and was hiding it in the creek next to the road. I pulled my sweater tight around my uniform and yanked the hair net from my head. I broke through the side hedge so I wouldn't have to walk past them.

"Hey, Kitty Lee!" called out Jessica. "Where are you running off to? Come on over and talk."

I stopped, taking time to arrange my face before turning around. Part of me wanted to march right over there so I could look Cody right in the eye and tell him I knew he was showing off with Jessica for *my* benefit and that it was duly recognized and recorded. I wasn't sure why it bothered me so much, but I had confused two orders mostly because I spent half my time looking out the window to see what Jessica and Cody were up to. Once, I gave a double dip twist to a three-year-old who could barely hold it, and next, I handed old Mr. Penrail a spicy chili dog. Afterward I remembered he had asked for a plain boiled hot dog. Right now that polite, kind man was probably searching through his bathroom medicine chest for a bicarbonate of soda. All because Cody was playing some sort of game with me. That wasn't like Cody. Even when we were little and playing Candyland and Spit and Chutes and Ladders, we always, *always* talked about the rules first.

Cody had tossed out the rules the night he started ignoring me at the Regent, and he had been playing wild ever since.

And now he actually thought I wanted to come over there so he could start another game?

"No, thank you." My voice had begun loud, but was barely above a whisper by the time I finished. Cody and Jessica probably didn't notice. They were both too busy staring at each other. Cody had his arm around Jessica's waist as if he were afraid she'd blow away. I watched as Cody slowly lowered his head and kissed Jessica, wondering if he did it in slow motion so I wouldn't miss a thing.

I didn't.

Aside from a few June bugs, I guess I was the only one who saw them kissing. It was a serious kiss, not like the spin-the-bottle kind we had all tried on each other years ago. I stood there watching until Cody broke away and looked over at me.

He stared at me like he knew I would be exactly

where I was. He didn't smile like it was a joke and he didn't look aglow like Dottie did when she talked about Ronnie.

He just looked right into my eyes like he had said something to me and was waiting for an answer.

Chapter Nine

I had so much trouble sleeping that night, I needed a can of Pepsi the next morning just to wake up.

Gramma set a glass of orange juice down in front of me with a thump. "Drop a nail in that poison you're drinking and it will decay," announced Gramma. "Imagine what it will do to your stomach."

"I don't do it every morning, Gramma. Is Pop up yet?"

Gramma grunted in reply and slid back into her chair. She folded her hands on her stomach and sighed. "I'm worried about your father. Last night he fell asleep right on the porch swing. If I hadn't heard it creaking, he would have been out there all night. Lord knows what the neighbors are thinking."

I took a sip of juice. Maybe I would ask Pop to

do something special tonight. "You playing Bingo tonight, Gramma?"

Gramma nodded, a small smile beginning. "All I needed last Wednesday was B-five. Winning was so close I could almost taste it, Kitty. I almost had me a toaster oven."

I glanced at the one we already had on the counter. "When I get off work today, Gramma, maybe I'll walk down to the hall and buy a card and play with you. Save me a seat by the fan, okay?"

The prospect of company sparked Gramma. She got up and poured herself another cup of coffee, pushing back a few stray hairs into her thick gray braid. "Sounds fine. Why don't you ring Dottie and ask her to come down? I haven't seen that girl in weeks. I remember when you two could hardly wait for Wednesdays. That Dottie could keep track of five cards at a time without ever breaking a sweat."

That Dottie! I wasn't about to tell Gramma that now Dottie was busy keeping track of five lies at a time. All because a stranger rode into town. And if he hadn't moved here and started planting some dumb hedges, he wouldn't be chasing Dottie. And if Dottie had been sitting with me at the movies, then I never would have sat with Cody. Then Cody would still be my friend and not kissing Jessica LaShay in broad daylight.

"What bug's biting you?" asked Gramma.

"Nothing, I guess I was just thinking about how life keeps changing." I stood up. "Gram, did you have any idea when you first got married that you would raise your own son and then turn around and raise his little girl, too?"

Gramma shook her head and patted my hand. "Seems like I was twice blessed."

"I know Momma was shorter and blonder and probably a whole lot prettier than me. But other than that, do I look at all like she did when she was sixteen?"

Gramma reached into the pocket of her robe and pulled out her reading glasses. She pushed them up on her nose, crossed her arms, and studied me like this was the sixty-four-thousand-dollar question.

"Spittin' image," she said at last.

I walked over and pounded on Pop's door. When I peeked in, he was already pulling on his socks.

"Hi, Pop."

"Hey, Kitty. I can't smell the bacon yet. Tell Gramma I'll be out soon."

Gramma banged the heavy black skillet on the stove and Pop and I both grinned. Gramma Belle only allows Pop three slices of bacon a month since he had his cholesterol test done. All the while she's cooking it she frowns and shakes her head like she's frying up hemlock.

I walked back into the kitchen and took a sip of Gramma's coffee.

"Did Momma like to cook?"

"Your momma took my chocolate walnut cookie recipe and turned it into a masterpiece." Gramma laughed. She lay the three thin strips of bacon in a row. She looked over at the closed bedroom door and took one of the strips back. "Why I remember her calling me to say she had to double the recipe every Friday night because so many people stopped by to talk."

"So Momma liked people?"

Gramma's smile froze a split second. "Lord, yes, she did . . . always wanted them around." Gramma grabbed a sponge and started to scrub the sink. "Most times," she repeated softly.

"What do you mean, 'most times'?" I hated to think that my momma had a temper. I wanted to hold onto the thought that she loved everyone and they loved her right back.

Gramma shrugged. "Your momma did like company, but all I'm saying is that sometimes she liked to just have her porch empty. That's all."

The kitchen was quiet. Gramma walked past me and tapped her sponge on my shoulder. "Now your father liked a full porch twenty-four hours a day. To hear him talk, everyone filled up the porch because of his stories."

"What stories?"

Gramma bent down and got out the toaster. "Your father knows every West Virginia story there is to tell." She frowned again at the closed bedroom door. "Boy, that seems like a century ago."

"Do you remember any of the stories, Gramma?"

"Oh, sure. But your pop can tell them best. If he still remembers them, that is. When your granddaddy was still alive, we would all go out on the porch, and your momma would carry you out and set you in a little white wicker basket, and we'd all start talking. Pretty soon, your father would start us laughing over something and before you knew it, the whole porch would be filled up with folks wondering what was so funny." Gramma had a far-off look in her eyes like she was trying to remember more. "And your momma was the one laughing the loudest. She'd be in the rocker, jiggling your basket with her feet and smiling at your pop like he was the brightest light she had ever seen."

I looked back over my shoulder, listening to Pop coughing inside the bedroom. He opened the bedroom door and stretched. Even with my eyes narrowed, it was hard to imagine him keeping a porch filled with his funny stories. Harder yet to imagine him as anyone's brightest light.

"Smells good," Pop announced as he walked in and poured himself a cup of coffee. "I hope I'm getting eggs this morning."

Gramma just grunted.

"Hey, Pop, why don't we meet Gramma down at Bingo tonight? I'll walk back after work and pick you both up. It would be fun."

Pop's eyes widened. "Bingo? Down at the hall with Gramma and her gang of desperadoes?"

I laughed. "Come on. Afterward we can all walk over to the diner and I'll treat for coconut cream pie."

"Speaking of pie, you two go on outside and see if the milk is here yet. I ordered whipping cream and it will go bad in a second in this heat."

Pop picked up his cup of coffee and followed me out on the front porch. I lifted the milk box lid: empty.

Pop sat down heavy in the swing, sipping his

coffee and rubbing his hand across his whiskers.

I hopped up on the railing and looked around the porch, trying to picture Momma in her rocker with my little basket at her feet. Pop probably sat in the swing so he could have a good view of his audience.

"Gramma was telling me about the good stories you used to tell, Pop. She said you could fill up a porch faster than anyone."

I almost hoped Gramma would turn off the bacon and come out now. That would make three of us on the porch. Almost like old times.

"Stories?"

Pop didn't look like he remembered, but that was only natural. He probably stopped telling them about the time Momma died.

"The stories you used to tell after supper, out here on the porch? Gramma said Momma would bake her chocolate walnut cookies and you would make everyone laugh and soon you had people sitting on the railing."

Pop grinned and sat up straighter. "Yeah, come to think of it, I did. Why, I remember Pete Rudderman laughed so hard one night he fell back and landed right on your momma's flowers."

"Gramma said I was out here, too, listening to you from my little wicker basket."

"Your momma and I found that basket at a garage sale two days before you were born. We didn't even have the crib set up yet, so you slept in there like a little puppy."

I was going to have to locate that basket. Maybe fix it up and put some geraniums in it and set it back on the porch. Why, it might do Pop good to start telling his stories again. Maybe then he wouldn't be so quick to jump back in bed when the stars are barely out.

"Maybe you could tell me a story on the way to Bingo tonight, Pop," I suggested. If I could get him back to telling his stories, maybe I could get him back to where he would want to fill up the porch again.

I felt that surge of energy that comes with party planning.

"I'm going to ask Gramma to dig up my wicker basket while I'm at Jake's, and you practice your stories."

Pop looked up, giving me a slow smile.

Things were going to be all right. I could see it all there, just waiting for me to organize it into being the way it used to be.

"See if you can remember Momma's very favorite story, Pop. Tell me that one first."

Pop's face clouded over then. The lights in both eyes went out quick like some fool had gone and pulled the plug.

Shoot! *I* was the fool. Why did I have to go and try to shove Momma into the middle of this? Every bit of liveliness drained right out of Pop, hunching him down a notch in the swing till he looked weighed down with the memories, years older than Gramma Belle.

He pulled himself slowly up with the chain of the swing.

Pop emptied the rest of his coffee over the railing and walked back inside. No one had to tell me he wouldn't be going to Bingo or to get a slice of that coconut cream pie.

Minding other people's business was like walking on eggshells. Here I was, sliding all over the floor with the mess I was making. My pop didn't want to talk to me about what was troubling him. Guess he didn't really need to talk as much as I needed to hear. I was sitting in the porch swing, going fast, when I heard a car door slam.

Mr. Bradley Curtis was coming up our walk. Before I even had time to close my mouth he was standing right in front of me like he did this every morning of his life.

"Morning, Kitty Lee."

"Morning, Mr. Curtis." I got up and kind of stood at attention, waiting for him to tell me what brought him all the way over here.

"I stopped by to talk to Jake this morning and he told me where you lived. I hope you don't mind."

I shook my head. Everybody in town knew where I lived; it wasn't a secret. The only secrets surrounding me were about Momma. And the way things were going, they would stay secrets forever.

Mr. Curtis shoved both hands into his pocket. He looked nervous and upset about something. Maybe something happened to one of the kids.

"I was wondering if you gave the baby-sitting job any more thought," he asked slowly. "The lady who's been helping out can't come back. She got a job offer in Cumberland that she was waiting for."

He trailed off in a defeated sort of way.

"I bet if you put an index card on the bulletin

board in Foodway, you'd get a lot of calls, Mr. Curtis."

He looked up, disappointed. "My children already know you, Kitty. It would be easier, less stressful than a total stranger."

I nodded my head. "Well, I'd like to help you, but I did promise Jake I would work right up through Labor Day. He's counting on me."

Mr. Curtis gave a lopsided grin. It made him look like Cody just then. "I'd be willing to throw in a two-hundred-dollar bonus if you just give it a chance. I talked to Jake, offered to pay for his want ads. He said if you're willing to stay till you train the new girl, he'd be glad to help out. He said he could manage okay without you."

"He did?" Part of me was surprised, the rest hurt that I was so dispensable. First Cody, then Pop and my best friend, Dottie — now Jake . . . everyone managing just fine without me.

"I'll even go down and help hose off the picnic tables and make the sloppy Joes."

We both smiled then.

"I really need you, Kitty," Mr. Curtis said quietly.

I could hear Pop and Gramma inside, arguing about the missing eggs.

"Please," he repeated.

I nodded then and whispered, "Okay." Why not? If Jake said he could do without me, then I guess he probably could. Just like Dottie and Pop and rotten old Cody.

The clock started to chime as the clouds shifted and the sun shone down directly behind Mr. Curtis, giving him a golden glow. The clock continued to strike as he explained what I would be doing with the children. I held out my hand for his business card and nodded at all the right places. I even remembered to smile as we shook hands on the deal.

Chapter Ten

My first three weeks baby-sitting at the Curtises' were a whole lot harder than rush hour at Jake's. No matter how hard I tried with Joey, he acted like war had been declared the moment I stepped foot in his house.

"I don't have to make my bed if I don't want to," he snapped every morning, throwing his pillow across the room. "And I don't have to listen to a thing you have to say." Most mornings I would calmly pick up the pillow, resisting a strong urge to whack it on his backside, and say, "Actually, Joey, you *do* have to listen to me. Until your momma is feeling better, I'm here to take care of you."

The little girls were another, more pleasant, story. They would run up to me the moment I walked in the house, full of fun and announcing they had already made their bed and brushed their teeth.

"Can you paint our nails now, Kitty?" asked Janice. She was almost six and followed me like a little shadow. I had finally got all the tangles out of her hair and it looked cute now in two fat braids.

Chrissy climbed on my lap with her little quilt. "Me, too."

"Sure, run and get the polish from my purse and some paper towels, Janice. I'll meet you out on the front porch."

"Stupid girls," Joey muttered as the girls raced down the stairs laughing. It sure sounded good to hear the girls so happy. They acted like having a momma laying in bed all day was the most natural thing in the world. Joey was the only one acting poisoned by the whole experience. Even Mr. Curtis would come home from work, smiling and bringing surprises for everyone. None for Mrs. Curtis, though. Sometimes he would even forget to ask if she got out of bed or came downstairs to talk to the children. Maybe he just got too used to the answer being no.

"Joey, I'll help you with the bed and then we'll have time to do something fun together."

Joey sat down on the window seat and pretended like he was reading a comic book. "You make the bed. My dad is paying you lots to baby-sit."

I sat down on the edge of the bed, holding the pillow in front of me like a shield. "I work harder here than I ever did at Jake's, Joey. Fact is, I'm thinking of charging an extra five dollars an hour unless you stop giving me such a hard time. I've been here three weeks and you haven't smiled once."

Joey's eyes peered at me over the comic book.

"I don't know why, either. I have two little cousins, just about your age, living right here in town and they think I'm a lot of fun. They smile at me fifty times a day." I stood up and started spreading out the sheet. "I guess it's because I'm pretty good at baseball and finding good fishing spots. Of course, maybe you don't have an interest in any of that."

"Yes, I do," Joey said fast. He dropped his comic and started tucking in the blanket. "Are they boy cousins?"

I nodded. "Yes, they are. In fact, I was just over there last Saturday to give them some lumber and nails I found in my garage. They're adding on to the clubhouse their big brother and I built years ago."

"Is it in a tree?"

"Sure is, an oak tree bigger than this house. They said I was welcome any time I wanted to come down and see their improvements."

"Well, I bet they wouldn't want me looking at it."

I ran my hand over the blue-checked bedspread, flattening out the ripples. "Well, I guess we could walk down in a bit and see. My cousins are real nice kids. You'll probably meet them once school starts."

"I hate school," muttered Joey.

"I never did like math," I confided. "But I love gym class. And I love finding out about new books."

Joey and I both glanced up at the shelf above

75

his bed, crammed full of books. Most of them had book markers keeping a place.

I started out the door with Joey following me. "Can we go after you paint the girls' fingernails?"

"Sure!" I said.

As I walked down the hall, I glanced over at Mrs. Curtis's closed bedroom door. Little snatches of radio music seeped out through the crack. I had been working there for weeks and I'd never seen her face. Every afternoon I would bring up a lunch tray and knock on her door, but she always called out to leave it outside. It was kind of spooky, like she was in a self-imposed jail right inside her own house.

"Don't worry about Mrs. Curtis," Mr. Curtis had explained the very first morning. "Your job is to take care of the children. I'll be home by five-thirty every afternoon and I will take care of my wife."

But I *did* fix Mrs. Curtis a tray, asking the kids to help me with it. I didn't want the kids to forget about her. Sometimes I had them sit down at the kitchen table and color their mom a pretty picture and we put that on the tray, too. Joey never would. "She isn't sick," he would whisper. "She's just pretending."

It wasn't my place to explain things to someone else's son, so I usually let it pass and eventually I stopped putting the paper and crayons in front of him. Part of me wondered how sick this woman was, too. Some days, I could hear her singing and the television blaring. Why was she having such a good time laughing with game show hosts when her own kids were downstairs without her?

One day, Joey said he wanted to draw her a picture. I almost knocked over the juice getting him a piece of paper before the urge left him. As soon as he picked up the pencil, Joey drew a monster with long red fingernails and dark glasses.

"That monster isn't Mommy," said Janice as she came up behind Joey.

"Yes, it is," said Joey with a trace of a smile. He added a small skunk. "Her room smells and it's dark like a monster's cave."

Janice looked down at her own rainbow. I had taught her the correct order of the colors and she made one almost every morning. In the center, she had printed: I LOVE YOU, MOMMY!!!

Joey looked down at Janice's picture.

"Your momma's going to feel better soon," I said. "Then she'll be able to play with you and take you to the park down by the river."

"No, she won't," Joey said simply. "I don't want her to, anyway."

"I do," Janice said.

"I do," Chrissy repeated, chewing on the end of a green crayon.

Joey added a small boy to his picture. Joey was a great little artist. The boy in the picture had ears, nostrils, and even curved eyebrows. He was wearing a baseball cap for the New York Mets. I stared at it for a long time, wishing Joey hadn't given the monster blonde hair. After he ran outside to play, I picked up the picture and studied it some more. Joey sure knew how to draw. It wasn't until I sat down with his drawing that I noticed that the little boy, so perfectly drawn, didn't have any hands.

Chapter Eleven

Both little girls were sitting on the front porch, waiting. I shook the Flamingo Pink polish and started on Janice's thumbnail. She was trying hard to stop biting her nails so they would be pretty when school started in September. I was just about finished with Chrissy's, leaving the thumb she sucked alone, when Joey came and sat next to us on the porch. He didn't frown or complain about everything like he usually did. I noticed he had a hammer laying next to him, but I didn't let on that I saw. I hoped that Cody's little brothers would ask Joey to help with the clubhouse. They probably would, since they were such nice little kids.

Thinking about Cody made an angry flash shoot through me so hard my hand shook and I smeared Flamingo Pink all over Chrissy's finger. I had forgotten that Cody might be over at the clubhouse, since it *was* in his backyard. Fact was, Cody's little brothers, Wayne and Jackie, weren't my real cousins at all. But since I had always spent so much time over there, I called Cody's mom aunt, and it just seemed fitting to think of the rest of them as cousins.

But since Cody had been dragging Jessica LaShay all over town, kissing her in broad daylight so often that even Gramma Belle had commented, I only thought of him as a fool.

I cleaned up the nail painting mess and went inside to pack some crackers, fruit, and cheese in case the kids got hungry on our hike over to the clubhouse. With any luck, Cody would be kissing Jessica somewhere else and I wouldn't have to look at his smart-alecky face.

We were halfway down Willard Avenue, cutting through the Brady yard, when we heard a car horn.

I had Chrissy piggyback and Joey and Janice were having a good time chasing each other with milkweeds, so we didn't even turn around.

Three honks later, I turned to see what the commotion was about. Mr. Curtis stuck his hand out the window of his car, waving. From the way he was smiling, you just knew how pleased he was to see his kids out running around in the fresh air like they were meant to do.

I shifted Chrissy up a hitch and cut through the lilac hedge. As soon as I climbed the grassy bank, I saw Cody. He was holding a ladder in place while his little brothers Wayne and Jackie hammered a PRIVATE sign in place.

Joey looked back at me with a scared look, as if the sign was meant for him.

"Hey, there, Wayne. Hey, Jackie! The sign looks good!" I called out.

All three of them turned around and looked. Right away, Wayne and Jackie broke into a smile and started coming down the ladder. Cody stared at me and then looked back at the sign. I ignored him.

"Joey, Chrissy, and Janice, I want you to meet my cousins, Wayne and Jackie."

"And that's my big brother, Cody," Wayne finished. "Did you find any more lumber, Kitty? We want to make a roof."

"I bet Pop would let you have that big piece of walnut paneling he has in the back of the garage," I offered. Pop had been keeping it in case of a water leak in the basement, but it had been there for twelve years or so already, just taking up space. "Maybe you boys can bring your wagon down later this afternoon, say about one-thirty, and Joey and I can help you load it up."

I went on talking a mile a minute like some sort of blue jay so no one would go and get shy on each other.

"I have a hammer," Joey said. "And there's a lot of wood in our basement left over from when the carpenter put in shelves in my dad's den."

"Wow!" cried Jackie. "Can we have it?"

Joey nodded, a small smile beginning to grow. "I bet I could get some nails, too. *Long* ones."

Once everyone started talking at once and looking for bugs and spiders in the fallen log next to the clubhouse, I walked over to talk with Cody. All of a sudden I really missed being good friends with him. Maybe it was because we were at the clubhouse we had both worked so hard on in the second grade.

"We had fun making this clubhouse, didn't we, Cody?" It might be best if we just ignored what had been going on for the past couple of weeks and started fresh.

"What do you mean, saying we're *cousins*?" snarled Cody in a hoarse whisper. "We aren't cousins! I'm not a bit related to you, Kitty Lee."

Cody was glaring at me like I had just lied before the Supreme Court. He tugged at the rope swing, wrapping it around his fist and yanking till his muscles stood out like bowling balls.

"Well, I do call your mom 'Aunt Karen,' and you call Gramma Belle 'Gramma,' and we've always kind of been like family and . . ."

"We were kids then," Cody said shortly. He reached down for a hammer and added another nail to the PRIVATE sign like he wanted to underline the fact.

I didn't say anything back.

"Can I climb the ladder, Cody?" asked Joey. His face lit up like a Christmas tree. "Please?"

It was nice to hear Joey talking so politely.

"Ask my *cousin*, she's in charge of you," Cody said curtly, before he turned and walked away.

I could have socked Cody right then and there. Couldn't he see how hard Joey was trying to be nice to everyone? Joey's face fell a thousand stories and went beet-red.

"You go on up, Joey," I said real quick. "Don't mind Cody any. He just woke up on the wrong side of bed, is all."

As soon as Joey scooted up the ladder, I walked

over to Cody and grabbed him by the arm, shoving him right into the weeds. "What's wrong with you, mister? Why are you being so mean to those little kids and trying so hard to make me look bad?"

Cody threw back his head and laughed. But any fool could tell his laugh was meant to be pure mean. If it had been in one of Joey's comic books, red flames would have been shooting out of his mouth.

"Yes, and I suppose you cared about how you made *me* look in front of our friends?" demanded Cody. "James and the guys sure gave me a rough time about you ditching me at the Regent, Kitty."

"What? Is that what you've been so mad about all this time?" I was truly having a hard time following all this. "Why would they tease you? I wasn't your date or anything. Cody, it wasn't like I was *with you*. I was sitting next to you, is all."

Cody snapped a stick in half. "That's right. I bought your damn ticket, but we weren't a date, were we? Cousins don't date, do they?"

Cody's voice got louder and louder until all the kids quieted down and were staring at us.

"Hey, Kitty, look at me up here," Joey said at last.

I smiled. I bet that was the first clubhouse Joey had ever set foot in.

"Can I have a drink, please?" asked Janice softly. She tugged on Cody's jeans. "I think I chewed up a bug."

I looked up at Cody, wondering if he was going to be mad at the whole lot of us.

"Sure," said Cody. "Come up to the house with me."

I sat on the log for almost an hour and watched Joey play. He was shouting orders to his imaginary troops, just like Wayne and Jackie. After a while Chrissy dropped her leaf collection and walked over to me. I pulled her on top of my lap. It wasn't long before she stuck her thumb in her mouth and leaned against me. I rubbed her back and started singing a little song about birds and flowers and sunny days. It wasn't all that fancy, just sort of the kind of song you make up as you go along.

My voice isn't real pretty and it will never get me center stage, so I was surprised to look up and see Cody watching me as if it were.

Chapter Twelve

"So what time did Pop finally get home?" I asked Gramma early the next morning. Dottie and I had gone out for pizza since Ronnie had to work late, and when I went to bed at ten-thirty, Pop still wasn't home.

"*Late*, he got in late," said Gramma, rubbing her eyes and yawning like she had carried him home herself. "I looked at the clock when I heard the commotion and it was past three. How he got himself here at all with all that liquor in him is beyond me. I'm sure his name is being mentioned at every breakfast table in town right now. His singing probably woke up half the street and then he carried on so on the front porch, probably woke up the other half. I'm surprised you didn't hear him."

The humidity had been so bad last night that I had turned my fan on high. Between the fan and being so exhausted from working till five at the Curtises', I slept nine hours straight.

Gramma took in a deep breath and jabbed at her egg like it was Pop himself laying on top of her toast. "I'm about wore out with that man. First he sleeps all the time and now he's out drinking with that trash down at Ernie's Bar and Grill. I swear I heard him telling one of his fishing stories last night out on the porch."

"But that's good, Gramma. Maybe he was telling one of his friends. That's a good sign."

Gramma shook her head while she chewed, then washed it all down with her juice. "Lord, Kitty. It isn't a good sign at all. He was alone on that porch. Your pop was talking to himself."

Well, that made me drop my fork all right. A guilt pang shot straight through me, wondering if I had stirred something up that should have been left settled at the bottom of the pond. Ever since I mentioned the stories that Momma liked hearing, Pop had been consumed with them. I saw bits of paper with snatches of them laying all over the house, like Pop was trying to jar his memory.

"Don't fret, Kitty. I told that man that he better snap out of it before this moodiness becomes a bad habit. He said he was just missing your momma, is all." Gramma reached across the table and patted my hand. "So now that he's admitted it, he'll come around."

Staring across the table at Gramma Belle, I felt a heap better. There was a lot of steel in that woman.

"I'll be home for supper today, Gramma. And don't forget that Dottie is spending the night here tomorrow."

Gramma nodded, dunking her crust in the yolk. "Seems like she spends the night here a lot lately, but she doesn't really spend much of the night."

I knew what Gramma was talking about. Two nights ago, Dottie and Ronnie went bowling but she didn't tiptoe back into my room until almost twelve-thirty. Everyone, including Gramma, knows Lucky Lanes closes at ten during the week. Then Dottie spent a long time in the bathroom, running the water, and when she came out her eyes were as red as could be. If love is supposed to be the best thing in your life, how come it makes so many people plain miserable?

Jessica LaShay was busy telling everyone in town that Cody and she are in love now. Jessica is as happy as always. She's been constant-in-love with somebody since she was ten years old. It's a permanent condition with her. But no matter what people say, Cody *wasn't* happy. He didn't put on a sad face just when I was looking, either, to make me feel guilty about Lord knows what. Lots of times I saw him walk past the diner or the five-and-dime when he didn't know I was on the other side of the window. And he looked terribly unhappy to me, like he had been kidnapped into this love affair and he didn't know how to find his way back home.

Gramma set her angel food cake tin right in front of me.

"Tell Dottie that if she gets in before nine, I'll have a fresh angel food cake waiting for her. I'll have a piece with her myself and we can catch up on old times."

"That's real nice, Gramma."

Gramma started pulling the flour tin and sugar sack out of the pantry. "Dottie always said that she wanted me to bake her wedding cake, remember, Kitty? Back when you two were still at the elementary school she made me sign that cute little contract that the cake had to be angel food."

Boy, did that seem like a long time ago.

"Dottie probably won't be in until midnight," I said carefully. The news disappointed Gramma all right. She always liked having a full table. If Dottie had any sense left she would have come and eaten Gramma's angel food cake instead of running down to Fort Ashby to be tempted by the devil himself.

It had been weeks and weeks and I still hadn't met Ronnie. Dottie's excuses got lamer and lamer until I finally stopped asking to meet him at all.

Gramma started wiping off the counters even though they were as clean as a whistle already. I knew she wanted to talk.

"Dottie is okay, isn't she, Kitty?"

"Oh sure. But she spends all her time with her new boyfriend."

Gramma smiled. "Isn't that nice. I always knew she would find a nice boy one day." Gramma grinned. "I'm happy for Dottie, aren't you?"

I took another bite of toast, pretending I was so consumed with chewing that I couldn't tack on an opinion of my own. Loyalty to Dottie stopped me from adding that I didn't know him from the holes in the ground he dug, and that he was probably only dating Dottie because he sensed she was desperate for love and would believe his lies.

"Well, I better get over to the Curtises'. Joey and Janice called me this morning and said they had a big surprise for me."

"That's nice." Gramma crossed her arms and looked carefully at me. "Now how come you don't have a steady fellow, Kitty? You get prettier every day, and I'm not the only one thinking it, either."

I rinsed my plate and put it in the dishwasher. "Guess I can't find one special enough, Gramma. Took you twenty years to find Granddaddy, didn't it?"

Gramma laughed. "Yes, it surely did, and they broke the mold when they made him, that's for sure."

As I walked to the Curtises' I wondered myself why I didn't love someone. Seemed the whole town was in love with somebody by mid-July. Of course, I didn't want to link up with someone just so it *seemed* like I was in love. I wanted to *be* in love. Just to see what it felt like, I told myself. Back then I didn't think love had to last. Of course, back then, I hadn't had my first taste of it.

Chapter Thirteen

"Guess what, Kitty Lee?" Janice ran down the front walk and hugged me around the waist. "Daddy's staying home from work all day and building us a clubhouse."

"We can paint it any color we want," added Joey from the side yard. "We've been up in the tree all morning."

Chrissy raced down the walk and grabbed my hand. "I'm a helper."

"I'm not even afraid up there," said Janice. "Do you want to help, Kitty?"

"Sure." I took the girls' hands and walked around back. Mr. Curtis was already up in a tree, nailing down the floorboards. A ladder leaned against the oak, with ropes and buckets dangling like wind chimes from the lower branches.

"Kitty, look, I put the nails in one bucket," said Joey. "And when Dad runs out, I just lower the bucket and fill it up again."

"And I put snacks in the other bucket in case Daddy gets hungry," added Janice.

The backyard, usually better groomed than most people's kitchens, was a mess. Lumber was piled by the rose garden, paint cans were stacked on the patio, and the kids' plastic wheelbarrow and tools were scattered around the tree. It looked messy and wonderful.

"Hello down there!" Mr. Curtis pushed back his baseball cap and smiled. "I hope you came to help."

"She did!" cried the children.

"Kitty knows all about clubhouses," Joey said proudly.

I nodded, my eyes still glued to Mr. Curtis, looking so handsome and casual in his blue jeans and T-shirt. He seemed relaxed and happy, as if all along it had been his seersucker suit making him so uncomfortable.

"What do you want me to do?" I put on the blue-checked work gloves Joey handed me.

Mr. Curtis pointed to the pile of two-by-fours. "I've finished the floor. Kitty, I guess we're ready for the side railings. Why don't you hand me up two smaller boards, honey?"

"Let me, Dad," said Joey quickly. "I'm real strong."

Mr. Curtis winked quick at me as I stepped aside and let Joey drag the board across the grass. Every few feet, Joey stopped, readjusted his grip, and grinned up at his daddy.

After all the railing boards were passed up, I gathered the tools into a neat pile by the patio.

"Maybe I'll go inside and get some cold drinks for you hard workers."

"And cookies," added Chrissy.

I went inside, turned on the radio, and started cleaning up the breakfast dishes. There were only four cereal bowls in the sink. On the counter was a tray with a slice of toast and a cup of coffee. Nothing had been touched. As I wiped out the sink, I glanced out the kitchen window. Joey had on the huge work gloves and was chasing his little sisters around the yard. The girls were laughing and screaming. Mr. Curtis was leaning over the clubhouse railings, waving his baseball cap each time the children made another lap around the tree.

They sure are having fun, I thought to myself. It was great to see everyone in such a good mood. Aside from the fact Mrs. Curtis never left her bedroom, things were getting much better at the Curtis house.

I loaded up a tray with lemonade and oatmeal cookies and walked out in the yard. "Anybody thirsty?" I hollered.

Mr. Curtis gave a phony Tarzan yell as he swung down from the lowest branch. He took the tray from me and led the way to a blanket under the tree. "This looks good. Thanks, Kitty."

We all sat down in the shade where we had a perfect view of the clubhouse.

"That is some great clubhouse, all right," I said. "You did a wonderful job, Mr. Curtis."

"It would look the goodest painted blue," Janice said seriously. "With a pink door."

"Or a yellow door," suggested Chrissy. "With sparkles."

"Ah, we don't need a door," said Joey. "Right, Daddy?"

Mr. Curtis studied the tree house and shook his head. "Anyone brave enough to climb that tree doesn't want to see a closed door when he finally gets up there."

"Or when *she* gets up there," I said quickly. I poked Chrissy and Janice. "Girls are the fastest climbers, right?"

The girls giggled. Mr. Curtis reached over and pulled Joey onto his lap. "No way. Joey and I are the fastest climbers in West Virginia."

Joey leaned back against his dad. "Yeah, maybe the whole world."

I scrambled to my feet, pulling Chrissy and Janice with me. "Says who?"

"Hey, let's clean up first," suggested Mr. Curtis. "Then I want to go into town and buy a flag for the new clubhouse. How does that sound?"

"Great!" shouted Joey. "Come on, guys!"

Mr. Curtis started walking across the yard, everyone hollering back and forth.

As Mr. Curtis bent to pick up the blanket, I raced over to the ladder and started climbing. "I think I'll make sure we didn't leave anything up here!" I laughed.

I was halfway up before Joey turned around and spotted me. "Oh, no, Dad, look! Kitty Lee's going to win."

Mr. Curtis dropped the blanket and raced back to the tree.

"No fair, Kitty. You'd better get down," he ordered in a deep voice. "Or else I'm coming up after you."

"First one up wins!" I called out as I climbed faster.

Down below the little girls were laughing and hopping around the tree. "Hurry up, Kitty Lee. Climb faster!"

As I threw my leg onto the platform, Mr. Curtis grabbed my left ankle. "Captured!"

"No way!" I was laughing so hard, I barely had the strength to kick off his grip. He reached over and grabbed both of my ankles, pulling me toward him. "I've got you now, Kitty. There's no way out."

"Get her, Daddy!" shouted Joey from below. "She's our prisoner!"

"Kitty won! Kitty won!" cried the girls.

"I did win," I said breathlessly. "Fair and square."

Mr. Curtis grinned and tightened his grip. "You cheated."

I shook my head and smiled back. "I did not. You got distracted is all."

Mr. Curtis stopped smiling for a second. His eyes looked right into mine. "Easy enough to do with you around, Kitty."

At first I wasn't quite sure what to say. Was Mr. Curtis still joking around, or was he telling me something else?

"Daddy, let me come up there!" cried Janice.

"Just a second, Janice," Mr. Curtis said quietly. He was still looking at me, his fingers wrapped tightly around my ankles. I could feel the heat of his fingers soaking right through my socks.

"Daddy!" wailed Janice. "I want a turn."

"I . . . we better . . ." My mouth felt so dry all of a sudden, the words were sticking in my throat.

Mr. Curtis was still just holding on to me. "I didn't think you were afraid of heights, Kitty Lee."

"I need a turn," shouted Joey from below. "I'm the oldest."

"I asked first!" shouted Janice. "Kitty, didn't I ask first?"

"Daddy!" Joey shouted. "I'm the oldest!"

"I asked first!"

Mr. Curtis was just looking at me, holding onto my ankles and waiting for something. "Are you afraid?" he asked again, his voice so low I wasn't quite sure what he was asking me.

"I'm not afraid. Just let your kids come up, Mr. Curtis." In the still summer air, my voice sounded shrill, like I was scolding Mr. Curtis.

Mr. Curtis let go of me and disappeared down the ladder.

Below me I could hear them all arguing. The children started to whine as they followed their daddy across the yard.

I started down the ladder myself, wondering what had happened.

At the bottom of the ladder, I picked up two plastic lemonade glasses and hurried toward the patio. It broke my heart to see the kids fussing, just when they were starting to enjoy each other.

"Hey, Mr. Curtis," I called out. "I just remembered something."

They all turned around. Chrissy took her thumb out of her mouth and wiped it on her shorts.

"If we get finished painting this clubhouse today, would you all like to go to the carnival over by the fairgrounds tonight?"

The kids started hopping up and down and laughing so hard, I knew Mr. Curtis didn't have a choice.

"Does that sound like fun?" he asked as he swung Chrissy up in his arms. "Anyone interested in cotton candy and the merry-go-round?"

"Yippee!" cried Joey. "That sounds real good."

I was glad to see everyone happy again. The way a family should be on a summer afternoon. I came up and stood next to them on the patio, searching Mr. Curtis's face to see if he was still mad at me.

But he kept his eyes on his children and his back toward me.

"Can we go right away, Daddy?" asked Janice.

"We'll go tonight," promised Mr. Curtis.

As soon as the kids ran back out to play, Mr. Curtis reached for his wallet. "I have to go to the office, after all. If I'm not back by five, take the kids to the fair without me."

The whole time he was counting out the money, Mr. Curtis kept his eyes down, away from me. He was mad all right. So mad he wanted to get as far away from me as he could. Since I wasn't quite sure what had happened, I felt funny about saying I was sorry. So I just took the money and walked inside to put it on the shelf by the sink. And when I came back out, he was gone.

Chapter Fourteen

We waited till almost five-thirty, but Mr. Curtis never came home. I had the kids all dressed up with warm sweatshirts tied around their waists so we could stay till after dark when things cooled down and they turned on the carnival lights. I knew the kids would love riding the merry-go-round in the dark. It was as close as you got to magic in Romney.

"Doesn't Daddy like the circus?" asked Janice, standing beside me at the front window.

"It's the carnival, dummy," said Joey. He was sprawled on a chair, leafing through the same comic book he had been staring at for the past hour.

"Let's go," Chrissy said cheerfully.

"You're right," I agreed, picking up my straw bag. I had packed peanut butter and jelly sandwiches, a damp washrag in a baggie for sticky hands, a box of bandages, and Mr. Curtis's forty dollars. "I'll bet your daddy got tied up at the factory. Maybe he'll drive over to the carnival and meet us there."

"Ah, that's a lie," grumbled Joey. "He doesn't even know where it is."

I tugged on Joey's hand. "I *don't* lie, mister. Now come on and let's have some fun. Have you ever eaten a hot dog on a stick?"

Joey surprised me by grinning back. "How about a cheeseburger on a stick?"

"How about us getting to that carnival before they run out of cotton candy?" I laughed.

We were all laughing as we went outside and got in the station wagon. I had taken a tray of hot soup and a grilled cheese sandwich to Mrs. Curtis at five, and she did say that it smelled good. I was hoping that she would eat something, but I wasn't about to bet a dollar on it. Mr. Curtis kept telling me his wife was seeing a doctor. But the truth was, I had never seen a doctor or a bottle of medicine around their house. Whatever sickness Mrs. Curtis had was wrapped with layers and layers of mystery.

The kids were so excited about the carnival, I got excited, too. The same family-owned carnival had been coming to Romney for the pasty twenty years, with the same acts and the same booths set up to rob you blind. But it *was* a carnival, it gave the local kids a job for three nights, and nothing smelled or sounded so good as a summer evening with rides, loud music, hot pretzels, and laughter.

As soon as I had parked and put Chrissy in the stroller, we bumped across the field and headed down the midway. Joey played Go Fish and won a rubber dagger, Chrissy begged for a balloon, and Janice won a plastic ring because the man beside the scale couldn't guess her weight.

For less than three dollars of Mr. Curtis's money, his kids were having a great time.

"Let's go see the merry-go-round," I suggested. The four of us were slurping on ice slushes.

"Can we go see the snake lady?" asked Joey. He had his hand on the stroller but his eyes were glued to the posters on either side of the aisle.

"It's all fake and trash, Joey," I said primly. My voice reminded me of how I had answered Mr. Curtis up in the tree house. I sounded exactly like Reverend Beesle, down at the Methodist church.

"But I still want to see her," Joey pointed out. "Maybe I won't think it's fake at all."

"Hey, here we are at the merry-go-round!" I said, extra loud. "They've got a rooster to ride and look at all those ponies."

Joey and Janice broke away and ran to the long line forming along the string fence. I laughed out loud. Kids were so easy to make happy.

"Looks like you're having fun."

My knuckles went white on the stroller. It was like seeing a ghost. There was Mr. Curtis, grinning and standing tanned and handsome in his shorts and white sweater like he came to the carnival every summer of his life.

"Daddy!" Chrissy started to climb out of the stroller.

"Hey, honey. Are you having fun?"

Mr. Curtis picked up his little girl and hugged her.

"Want to ride the merry-go-round?" After

Chrissy nodded, Mr. Curtis took her to the other children. I just stood there and watched, smiling and nodding like I was witnessing a reunion of a family separated for twenty years, instead of just a few hours.

Once all the kids were strapped to their ponies, Mr. Curtis came back and stood beside me.

"Thanks for bringing them, Kitty. Look at their faces."

We both watched in silence for several minutes, waving as they spun slowly past us.

"They think they're really going somewhere, don't they?" I laughed.

Mr. Curtis put his arm around my shoulder and gave it a light squeeze. "But they are, Kitty," he said softly. "They are."

Before I could even turn to him, the music blasted louder and the merry-go-round stopped. Mr. Curtis hurried to the kids, unstrapping them and laughing as they all talked at once.

After we all shared a huge bag of cotton candy, Joey insisted that his daddy win him a teddy bear.

"Joey, those booths are the biggest rip-off in the world," declared Mr. Curtis. "They buy the bears for two dollars and people spend ten dollars trying to knock down little bottles to win them. It's a racket."

Joey looked so disappointed, I had to speak up.

"But of course, Joey, if the person trying to knock down the bottles has any real *talent*, then he can win himself a two-dollar bear for a quarter."

"What?" Mr. Curtis stopped dead in his tracks, making all sorts of funny faces. The kids and I were laughing so hard we couldn't walk.

"Kitty Lee can win me a bear then," Joey decided.

"For a quarter," laughed Janice.

Mr. Curtis held up both hands like a traffic cop. He reached in his pocket and handed me a quarter. "Here you are, bright eyes. You win a bear with this and. . . . and . . ."

"And you'll what?" I teased.

"I'll dance all night with the bear," laughed Mr. Curtis.

We walked down the game-booth aisle, passing the goldfish booth, the dart board, and the bottle hoops.

"Maybe they don't really have a teddy bear booth," said Joey.

"They've had one every year for the past twenty," I told him. They hired local kids to run it so I knew it wasn't rigged.

"There it is," cried Mr. Curtis. He took Joey's hand and hurried ahead. "I'll save you a spot, Kitty Lee."

"Better get your dance card ready," I hollered back.

By the time the girls and I arrived there were already about ten people gathered around the booth. Mr. Curtis was grinning and scribbling something down on a little white square tablet.

"What's your daddy doing now?" I asked.

"Being happy," said Janice. She looked up at me and put her hand in mine.

I pushed the stroller up and tapped Mr. Curtis on the shoulder. "What are you up to, Mr. Curtis?"

Lots of people started laughing.

"I'm waging a few bets, Kitty Lee. I say that

you can't knock down one bottle with your three balls. Some of these people agree with me, and some of them say you can."

"What?" I put my hands on my hips and acted like I was real insulted. Truth was, I wasn't at all. It was all just carnival talk. I waved to a few of the kids from the high school.

"I'm going to knock down all of the bottles with three balls, thank you very much," I said saucily, grinning as the crowd started to laugh.

Mr. Curtis dug in his wallet. He pulled out a fifty-dollar bill, kissed it, and passed it under my nose. "And here's fifty dollars saying you can't, sweetheart, so what do you say to that?"

Joey and Chrissy grabbed my hands and started jumping up and down. "She can do it, she can do it."

A few men in the crowd reached into their wallets and started talking to Mr. Curtis about his bet.

"Just let me at those bottles," I said, pretending to roll up my sleeves. I walked toward the booth, feeling people smack me good-naturedly on the back as I passed. "Let me see the bear that Mr. Curtis will be dancing with tonight."

As I stepped up to the booth, I almost swallowed my heart. There was Cody Baines, wearing a silly-looking yellow apron and a frown, his fist squeezing those three orange balls so tightly, I was afraid his knuckles would fly right out and knock me in the head.

Chapter Fifteen

"What in hell do you think you're doing?" Cody hissed.

I pushed my quarter toward him. "I'm having fun." I looked down and smiled at Janice instead of looking into Cody's mad face.

"She's going to win a bear and Daddy's going to have to dance with it," replied Janice.

"Okay, all bets in," announced Mr. Curtis. He moved through the crowd and stood beside me. I was surprised that a few of the men in the crowd already knew Mr. Curtis, maybe from the factory. One large man with curly red hair called him "sir."

Mr. Curtis put a dollar bill down on the counter and pushed it toward Cody. "Here you go. Give the lady her balls and let the contest begin."

Cody ignored Mr. Curtis's dollar and thumped three balls down in front of me.

"Why, thank you, sir," I said good-naturedly.

"Good luck, Kitty!" cried Janice.

"Hey, you better knock them down, lady," called a woman's voice from the rear. "I've got fifty cents saying you can."

Mr. Curtis pushed up both his sweater sleeves and leaned against the booth. He had one hand on top of Joey's head and held Chrissy in his arms. But he was smiling at me. He wasn't mad anymore and I was glad. It made me feel good to see how many people were warming up to him.

"If you're waiting for the drumroll, you're out of luck, Kitty," snarled Cody. "I had to let the band go."

Everyone started hooting and laughing then. I looked up at Cody, expecting him to grin, too, since he loves center stage. But Cody looked madder than ever. He was drumming his fingers against the counter and taking turns glaring first at me and then Mr. Curtis.

Janice tugged on my shorts. "Hey, that's your friend, Kitty," she whispered loudly. "From the clubhouse."

I picked up the first ball and shook my head. A friend was what Cody *used* to be. Not anymore. I let the first ball whip, knocking off the first two bottles of the five bottle pyramid. Some of the crowd started to clap, but I could hear some deep voices booing. Mr. Curtis just leaned his head to one side and smiled.

Cody leaned forward and pushed another ball in front of me. He wasn't trying to be helpful. He probably wanted me to just hurry up and get away from his booth.

"Knock them all down, Kitty!" Janice urged.

"Come on, honey, you can do it!" a lady hollered. "Show these men who's got the best arm!"

"You've sure got the biggest mouth, Diane," shouted another man.

I started to laugh myself then, making my second ball whack loudly against the heavy curtain behind the bottles.

"Kitty!" Janice leaned her forehead against the counter.

Before the crowd could add their two cents' worth, I picked up the third ball, squinted my left eye, and threw with all my might. Direct hit! The remaining three bottles sprayed out in all directions.

"You did it!" cried Janice.

"You won, Kitty!" laughed Joey, forgetting whose side he was on and running over.

I was smiling at the crowd and rubbing my arm when Mr. Curtis spun me around and hugged me. "Fair and square all right," he laughed.

I was so happy I hugged him back. "Let's pick out your dance partner, Mr. Curtis."

But we didn't have time for that. Before Mr. Curtis or I had time to turn around, Cody Baines was shoving a blue, three-foot bear in between us.

"Hey, thanks!" said Mr. Curtis, grabbing onto the bear and reaching out to shake Cody's hand.

But Cody ignored the outstretched hand. He slid his hands deep into his back pockets and stared darkly at me like he was searching the face of a stranger.

104

Chapter Sixteen

It was almost ten o'clock when we left the carnival, so Mr. Curtis ended up taking the kids home by himself. I couldn't believe it when he handed me the keys to the Mercedes.

"Gosh, Mr. Curtis, are you sure about trusting me with something so valuable?" I asked as I slid behind the wheel.

But Mr. Curtis just tugged on my ponytail and laughed. Then he got real serious and said, "Besides sweetheart, I trust you with what I truly hold most precious, every day."

I like seeing a man who isn't afraid to talk about how much he loves his kids. It made me respect Mr. Curtis a lot. On the ride home, it made me a little sad, too. It would have been so nice to have a momma that cared that much about me. A momma who would call up all her friends and brag in a soft way about my English papers or the nice way I could handle kids.

The next morning, I pulled slowly into the Curtises' driveway and parked the car in the detached three-car garage. It was a beautiful morning and I was glad to see paint cans and newspaper set next to the clubhouse tree. Maybe Mr. Curtis was going to stay home this morning and start painting. I was just about to step on the patio when I heard a crash and shouting from the second-story window.

Through the lace curtains of the master bedroom, I could see Mr. and Mrs. Curtis, nose to nose, shouting and waving their hands back and forth to beat the band. They both looked like they should have been standing in Ernie's Bar and Grill parking lot on a hot Saturday night, instead of upstairs in the biggest house in Romney.

"Give it back, Bradley, I *need* that."

"Always what *you* need, Elaine, right? Do you ever think about what your sick needs are doing to the children? To me? You shut yourself up here with this poison and . . ."

Right about this time, Mr. Curtis stopped in mid-sentence, as if someone had poked him in the back and pointed to the yard. He looked down at me angrily before he slammed the window shut.

I felt like a fool, like a little kid caught with her hand in the cookie jar. I hurried inside the kitchen where the kids, each one wearing a sad look, sat at the kitchen table. "Good morning, kids," I said cheerfully. "Didn't we have fun last night at the carnival?" The blue bear was sitting on a kitchen chair next to Janice. I could still hear yelling from upstairs so I flicked on the radio by the sink. "Hey, now. Finish your cereal and then we can go for a walk."

I sure hoped Mr. Curtis didn't think I'd been outside trying to eavesdrop on him and his wife. I mean, it hadn't been like I was lying flat under the rhododendron bush, just hoping to catch an earful. They were probably both mad that I had been staring up at the window.

"Kitty Lee! Why do they fight all the time?" asked Joey quietly.

"They fighted last night after we came home from the carnival, too," added Janice. She leaned over and hugged the bear. "Mommy said we were bad to go to the carnival."

"Hey, all people fight sometimes," I said. I picked up Chrissy, who buried her face in my neck right away. "I know . . . let's all go outside and make sure we have enough paintbrushes for the clubhouse."

Joey tried to smile. "Can I stir the paint?"

I reached over and hugged him. "Everyone can."

"First thing, let's go to your cousins' clubhouse," said Janice. "We can see if we forgot anything to put on our clubhouse. Daddy can build it today."

Joey frowned. "Yeah, except now that Daddy's fighting with Mom, he'll go back to work. Just watch."

I opened the back door, then closed it. You could hear Mr. and Mrs. Curtis yelling even more outside. "I've got a better idea," I said quickly. "Let's make a list of all the supplies we have to pack for the clubhouse. Like, crackers, and juice, and things like that."

I was relieved the kids liked my idea so much. I closed the kitchen door leading to the dining room and swung Chrissy back on her chair. "Let's make a list right now."

I had just got them settled, when Mr. Curtis pushed open the kitchen door and stuck his head in. "Kitty Lee, could I see you for a minute, please?"

All the kids looked up at me, so I smiled like I could hardly wait to hear what Mr. Curtis had to say. I pushed open the door and followed him into the foyer.

When he turned around, I saw that his hand was bleeding something fierce.

"Mr. Curtis, what happened?"

Right off he started to hide his hand from me, just like I was one of the kids. I reached for his hand, gently taking off the bathroom towel he had wrapped around it. The towel was already soaked with blood, and the palm of Mr. Curtis's hand was filling up with more blood like a bowl.

"Your finger is cut clean through, Mr. Curtis," I said. My voice was shaking as badly as my hands.

"It will be okay. I broke the bathroom glass and . . ."

I didn't even pretend to believe him. I turned and raced back into the dining room, pulling open drawer after drawer of the huge sideboard till I found a stack of neatly ironed linen napkins. I grabbed a stack and shook them out. They were white and clean and would stop the bleeding till I was able to get him to the hospital.

"I'll get the car keys and get you to the hospital fast before you lose too much blood," I said as I wrapped the wound. The cut was so deep the blood gushed out in spurts.

Mr. Curtis sat down on the bottom step and I held his hand up higher than his heart. "Wait here till I get the kids ready."

Mr. Curtis started to shake his head. "No, I'll be fine." But blood was already trickling down his arm so he just closed his eyes and reached in his pants pocket for the car keys.

If the Oscar people in Hollywood had been sitting in the Curtises' kitchen, they would have handed me a trophy on the spot. I rushed in all happy, rinsed my hands in the sink, and announced that their dad had cut his hand on a glass. They got to stay with Gramma Belle and have fun while I took him to the hospital.

Joey was the only one who started asking a hundred questions, but I finally got the kids all settled in the backseat. Then I draped a trench coat over Mr. Curtis's bloody hand and helped him into the front seat. I threw the car in gear and raced out of the driveway so fast Joey leaned over and started buckling his sisters up with seat belts.

I turned on the radio loud so nobody would start asking questions and tore through town, barely stopping at stop signs. Mr. Curtis just leaned his head against the window and by the time we pulled up in front of Gramma Belle's he had his eyes closed tight against the pain.

I herded the kids out and up the stairs, calling for Gramma Belle as soon as I hit the porch.

"Hey, Gramma," I said in a rush. "Look who's

here to help bake cookies. Mr. Curtis cut his hand and I'll be back as soon as I can."

Gramma's mouth was still hanging open by the time I hopped the hedge and slid back behind the wheel.

The car was spitting gravel as I sped down Locust, glad the hospital was only a few blocks away. It wasn't until I had run the second stop sign that Mr. Curtis slumped against my shoulder and fainted.

Chapter Seventeen

After Mr. Curtis was whizzed away on a gurney, I went out in the hall and called Gramma Belle to check on the kids. I wanted to make sure they weren't worried about their daddy. Gramma said they were fine and out back playing on the next-door neighbor's swing set. She was just about to whip up a batch of cookies for them. I told her Mr. Curtis was wheeled up to surgery because his little finger was hanging by a thread and he had already lost so much blood he looked whiter than a sheet. Mr. Curtis had bled like a stuck pig. No bathroom glass could have done all that damage. It was my guess that maybe Mrs. Curtis had a knife hidden up there and she attacked Mr. Curtis for hollering at her. I wondered if I should call the police.

Something fishy was going on in that house, all right. Mrs. Curtis didn't just have iron-poor blood or a weak heart. Maybe she was pure insane and should be locked up at Terrance State Hospital before she went running through the streets of Romney.

Ordinarily I would have felt sorry for her, sorry for anyone so tangled up with being mean. She was probably angry that Mr. Curtis and the kids weren't feeling as miserable as she was anymore. She was probably mad as a hornet listening to all the singing and laughing that had just got started in the house again. When I started working at the Curtises' the whole family was like some huge plant that was drying up from lack of proper care. Once I started laughing and playing with those kids, they just bounced back. That's probably why she stabbed her husband, to remind him of the pain she was carrying around inside. I didn't want to think that maybe the reason she stabbed him was because she saw him hanging onto my ankles and looking into my eyes up in the clubhouse.

I jingled the change left in my hand and half wondered if I should call Mrs. Curtis and let her know where her family was, and how Mr. Curtis all but bled to death in their fancy white car. But I didn't. I didn't understand the woman and unChristian as it sounded, it seemed to me that the lady wasn't worth the quarter for the call.

I had already read every magazine in the waiting room and was leafing through *Senior Years Lamplight*, when the doctor came in to talk to me.

"Are you with Mr. Curtis?" he asked.

"Yes, is he all right? Is he going to lose his finger?"

The doctor sat down and shook his head, but slow as if to show it wasn't too far from the truth.

"I'm not sure if there will be nerve damage. He's on the second floor now if you want to go up and see him. If I were you, I'd make sure he didn't get near that saw again till someone teaches him how to use it."

I just nodded, not wanting to mention that I had gotten a broken bathroom glass story.

My heart was having a regular tap-dancing marathon inside my chest as I took the elevator up to the second floor. Now that the worst was over I realized how terrible things could have been if I hadn't been there. Mr. Curtis might have just wrapped another scarf around his hand and gone on about his business. Then he would have fallen down, weak as a kitten, and bled to death in front of his scared little kids. I could feel my fist clench up as I thought about Mrs. Curtis, locked away in her bedroom doing Lord knows what, while her family was left to fend for themselves.

I marched down the hall like a general tramping across the battlefield to check on his wounded. I would take care of them all, Mr. Curtis and the kids. They were counting on me to help them fix up their lives, I just knew it. If I were to take the easy way out and mind my own business, it would be like turning my back on the whole bunch of them. I was going to get Mrs. Curtis out of that bed and let her know that she had a responsibility and she'd better face up to it before it was too late.

I pushed open his hospital door, peeking inside to make sure the nurses weren't doing something personal. Mr. Curtis lay sleeping, his cheeks as pale as the pillowcase. An I.V. tube ran from a pole, down into his arm. His hand was encased

113

in a huge bandage, propped up like he was all set to wave.

Poor Mr. Curtis. He looked so worn out with his three little kids and a wife who had probably tried to murder him with a kitchen knife. A wave of sadness swept over me like a sudden dust storm, leaving my heart so uncovered it scared me. I leaned over him, patting his free hand. He was cold as ice.

His eyes fluttered, then opened.

"You're going to be fine," I said automatically.

His good hand reached out and took mine. He closed his eyes again and held on tight. He started to smile then, pulling my hand up to his lips.

"Dear Kitty," he whispered. Then he brushed his lips against my hand. "Thank you for being there. What would I do without you?"

His hand fell back to the sheet, still holding onto mine. I didn't want to disturb him anymore, so I let my hand stay with his for a long time before I gently took it back.

Chapter Eighteen

As soon as I left the hospital, I took the car to a coin-operated car wash and tried to clean it up a little. I didn't want to scare the kids when I picked them up. I drove the Mercedes slowly down Main Street, my fingers gripping the steering wheel so tightly my back teeth hurt. I kept the speedometer between fifteen and twenty miles per hour. It wasn't so much that I wanted everyone to sit up and take notice of me in such an expensive car. It was more like I was scared stiff I would ram right into the back end of somebody's station wagon.

I wanted to go back to the Curtis house first, before I picked up the kids. I guess I wanted to make sure Mrs. Curtis hadn't done anything scary like slashing her own wrists or setting fire to the house.

I didn't bother to knock. As soon as I walked in, the quiet told me that Mrs. Curtis was probably still up in her room. I tried to make as much noise as I could pounding up the stairs, but it was kind of hard, since the carpet was so thick.

I stopped outside her door, knowing I had to go in there and try to talk some sense into the woman. Somebody had to let her know that things couldn't go on like they had been. I strode right in there. A little shiver went over me as I looked down at the bedside table. Next to the beautiful cut-glass lamp and porcelain picture frame, was a bottle of whiskey. The bottle was almost empty. Mrs. Curtis saw me looking, her eyes following mine.

"It calms my nerves," she said simply. She ran her hands through her tangled blonde hair and tried to shake it back off her shoulders. She must have been pretty once, but most of it had been erased. The dark circles under her eyes seemed almost theatrical.

"I took your husband to the hospital," I explained. "His hand was cut so badly they had to operate. They were able to save his finger."

Mrs. Curtis sat up straighter and looked positively green.

"The doctor said he can come home the day after tomorrow, Mrs. Curtis."

Maybe worrying about someone else might do her some good. Mrs. Curtis started coughing something terrible, like she was choking on something. Gramma Belle would have said it was her own guilt. But I ran to the bathroom to get her a glass of water. As I let the cold water run, I deliberately looked inside the trash can. There must have been three or four whiskey bottles broken up in there, maybe more. Maybe Mrs. Curtis had cut Mr. Curtis with one of them.

When I came back in with the water, Mrs. Curtis was trying to stand up. I'm not sure if it was the whiskey or the weakness in her knees that caused her to sway this way and that like a young willow tree.

"Where are my children?" she asked, grabbing onto the chair near the desk.

"With Gramma Belle at my house."

Mrs. Curtis nodded, then covered her mouth with both hands like she was going to be sick.

"Can I help you, Mrs. Curtis?"

She shook her head, her eyes angry that I was flaunting my own strength. Her thin peach night-gown was wrinkled, the rich ivory lace hanging unevenly at the hem.

"I'm just about to go pick up the kids and then I'll be glad to feed them supper and spend the night," I offered.

Mrs. Curtis's head jerked up. She blinked several times and stared at me again as if I had just stepped out from behind the curtains. "Where are my children?"

I rolled my eyes, not to make fun of her, but I was tired, myself. But Mrs. Curtis must have seen the look. She slid down onto the desk chair and pointed her finger at me. "Don't you dare look down your nose at me. What do you know about me or this family? Nothing!"

Mrs. Curtis's anger must have given her some strength, because she yanked open a drawer and pulled out a pair of jeans and a sweatshirt. She pulled her underwear drawer out so quickly, it shot out like a rocket, spraying panties and socks across the floor. Mrs. Curtis scrambled across the mess, picking up what she needed. "I will go get my own children and pick up my own husband, thank you very much," she whispered rapidly.

I knelt down beside her, refolding what I could. Mrs. Curtis just glared at me as she tore off her nightgown and started to dress.

"I don't mind picking up the kids, Mrs. Curtis," I said softly. I could tell by the way her hands were shaking that she wasn't in any shape to drive a car.

"I will pick my family up," she said. As she picked up her sweatshirt, she stopped, turning to me and going white as a sheet. Before she could say another word, she covered her mouth and raced for the bathroom. I could hear her vomiting.

I went into the bathroom and turned on the cold water. I soaked one of her hand towels and held it out to her. Her shaking hands reached for it.

"Thanks." She sounded so weak. She pressed the towel to her forehead for a second before she threw it on the floor and started wretching again. Her blonde hair hung down as she gripped the toilet. I could hear her crying as she vomited. I bent down and took her hair, smoothing it back and away from her face like Gramma did for me when I had the flu.

After a few minutes, Mrs. Curtis picked up the towel and leaned her head against the sink.

"Is he okay?" she finally asked.

"Yes," I said, handing her another damp towel.

"The doctor said he would be fine. You could probably call him and talk to him yourself."

She gave a harsh laugh. I let her hair fall and went over and started the shower. I laid a thick white towel across a small brass stool in front of her dressing table. "Take a shower, Mrs. Curtis. It will make you feel better."

I steeled myself for the angry look she would surely shoot me when she finally raised her head. But she never looked up. She stared at the floor the whole time she was pulling off her jeans and walking into the shower. She lifted her face toward the warm spray and I gently closed the glass shower doors. After a minute or two I opened them again and poured two capfuls of pink shampoo into her hand.

I sat on the toilet, kind of lifeguarding, while she showered for twenty minutes. It was quiet except for the water splashing against the doors.

Mrs. Curtis finally slid open the doors and wrapped herself in the thick white towel. Even soaking wet, she looked better coming out than she did going in.

"What is your name again?" Mrs. Curtis wiped the steamy mirror with her hand. As she leaned closer, she shuddered and turned her back on her reflection. "Carol Lee?"

"Kitty Lee Carter. Your husband hired me to help with the kids since . . ."

"I know."

"You have nice kids, Mrs. Curtis." She looked so sad all of a sudden. I wanted to say something to cheer her up a little. She was staring at the broken glass in the trash can like she didn't know how it got there and was afraid to ask. Mrs. Curtis picked up her hairbrush and started raking it through her hair. "Yes, I do have nice children, a nice house, a nice, handsome husband . . ." She trailed off, letting the brush clatter on the vanity top. She turned and faced me again. "So what more could a woman ask for, Kitty Lee?"

"Can I get you some soup?"

She laughed. "Soup won't do it, kid." She walked back into the bedroom with me following her. We both looked at the whiskey bottle at the same time. I walked over to the bed and fluffed up her pillows and pulled up the blanket. Maybe she wouldn't go back to bed if I made it. "Let's go downstairs, Mrs. Curtis. You could sit out on the patio in the sun while I go pick up the children. They would be so happy to see you outside, admiring their clubhouse."

Mrs. Curtis turned and raised an eyebrow. "Yet, gladder still to see you, right?"

"Of course not," I said quickly. Maybe too quickly because my cheeks burned fire-red and my voice didn't sound like my own.

"Actually," she said wearily, "I think I'll just rest up in my room for a little bit." She walked to the edge of the bed and sat down. "I'll read."

"Fine. I'll only be gone fifteen or twenty minutes." I turned on her light, and while I was there, I stuck the bottle of whiskey under my arm like it was just some knickknack out of place.

"I'll bring up some iced tea for you before I leave, and if I know Gramma Belle, she's already filled your kids full of fried chicken. I'll bring you

120

back a leg if there's any left. Or would you like a breast?"

I could tell by the way she put her hand over her mouth again, real fast, that the idea of fried chicken didn't really appeal to her right then.

She watched me walk to the door. Actually, she stared at the whiskey bottle tucked under my arm. We both knew the bottle was leaving.

"Dry your hair and maybe you'll feel like watching the kids play on the new jungle gym. They like to do tricks. I bet they'd like to show you them, don't you think?"

Mrs. Curtis was already crawling up on top of the spread to the pillows. But she wasn't saying no.

I closed the door and walked quickly down the stairs. In the morning I would be able to report to Mr. Curtis that his kids were just fine and that Mrs. Curtis had been up, showered, and read a nice book. He'd feel great knowing that things were progressing so nicely on the home front.

I picked up the car keys, jingling them, and anxious to get started. Once I picked up the kids, I'd let them play for a little bit, and then maybe we could grill hot dogs and roast marshmallows. For an extra little treat, I'd let them stay out till dark and catch lightning bugs. Afterward, I'd soak them in a bubble bath and we'd all call Mr. Curtis to say good night.

I closed the front door and started down the wide red-brick walk. When I glanced up to the second floor, I noticed Mrs. Curtis's blind had been drawn again. That woman didn't care a hoot about the treasures she had right under her own nose. By the time I was at the car, I had decided that as soon as I got the kids home, we'd call Mr. Curtis right then and there. We'd let him know we were all doing fine and that the children really missed him. We all did.

Chapter Nineteen

It wasn't until early the next morning during breakfast that I remembered about Dottie.

"Oh, shoot!" I cried as I spilled half the milk I was trying to pour over Chrissy's cornflakes.

"That's okay, Kitty," laughed Janice. "We spill stuff all the time."

"Thanks, Janice, but I just remembered my friend was suppose to spend the night with me last night and I slept over here with you all."

"I liked catching lightning bugs," said Joey. "I caught eight."

"Me, too," said Chrissy with a nod.

"No, sir, you only caught two, Chrissy," reminded Janice.

Chrissy just smiled like that didn't matter at all.

I hurried right over to the phone. I sure hoped Gramma Belle hadn't forgotten about Dottie coming and locked the screen door last night.

It must have rung ten times before Dottie's

mom finally picked it up. She sounded like she had just lifted her head from the pillow.

I tried hard to lower my voice. "Is Dottie there?"

"No, I'm sorry. She spent the night over at Kitty Lee's." I could hear her yawning. "She should be back soon."

I hung up, wondering if I would worry Gramma by calling her next. It was seven-thirty. Hopefully, Dottie was having some scrambled eggs with Gramma right now.

"Hello?"

"Good morning, Gramma." I couldn't believe how natural my voice sounded. Inside my heart was beating so fast my ears were pounding.

"Is Dottie up yet?"

There was a pause, just long enough to let me know that Dottie wasn't there to get up.

"Now, Kitty, Dottie never did come by." I heard Gramma return her cup to the saucer with a rattling clank. "I thought you called her and told her not to come. Lord, maybe I should call her mother right now and check."

"Wait, Gramma, don't bother doing that. I have to talk to Dottie anyway, so I'll just call. I bet she heard all about Mr. Curtis and knew I'd be staying overnight here. News travels lickety-split through Romney."

"Maybe so. Hey, are you bringing the kids over today? I thought we could pack a picnic lunch and head down to the creek. I bet those kids have never seen a real salamander before. I'm just putting in some bread to bake now. I can't remember when I had the oven going this early."

I looked up at the clock and smiled. Gramma

124

sounded as excited as the kids were going to be.

"Maybe you can keep an eye on the kids while I run down and see how Mr. Curtis is doing. He sounded awfully sad last night on the phone. He could hear the kids laughing and he said it made him want to crawl right through the wires to be with us, I mean them, the kids, of course."

I tugged at the phone wire and felt my cheeks blazing. Actually Mr. Curtis *had* said he wanted to be with us, but he meant his kids, probably.

"Kitty Lee," said Gramma. "I don't think you have to go over to the hospital. I mean, he is paying you to look after his kids, not *him*." Gramma gave a little laugh at the end, but she sounded the same serious way she did when she told me to take cover during a thunderstorm, or never to hitchhike along Highway 28.

"The poor man is lonely, is all," I tried to explain. "He doesn't know anybody in town really."

Gramma huffed at her end. "Well, plenty of people know who *he* is and it's a little embarrassing to have people coming up to me asking how come I'm letting you spend so many hours up at such a troubled house."

"Gramma!" I was shocked to hear her talking like that. I knew she loved those little Curtis kids as much as I did. And all the trouble was coming from Mrs. Curtis. I put my hand over the phone, knowing how hurt the kids would be to know people in town were already passing judgment on them.

"You never said anything about it before," I said carefully.

Gramma drew in a deep breath. "Well, to tell

you the truth, I guess I should have waited to talk to you when you were right across the kitchen table from me. But the shock of hearing it last night at Myrna's Tupperware party nearly knocked me off my chair. Myrna's older boy works up at the hospital, and I guess Mr. Curtis told one orderly he cut his hand on a saw and told the girl with the gift cart he fell on a bathroom glass, and the nurse in the operating room swears that it looked like somebody had cut him hard with something ragged."

"So?" So why should I stay away from taking care of these kids? I felt like asking.

"Then, that nosy Loretta came right out and said that she sure wouldn't trust any young girl around a man as handsome and as unhappily married as Mr. Curtis."

"None of them knows what they're talking about," I said simply. I wanted to hang up the phone and pretend I hadn't heard a thing.

After I got off the phone, I did the breakfast dishes and sent the kids up to make their beds and brush their teeth.

I made a pot of tea and some toast for Mrs. Curtis. She had been real quiet last night, but she had come downstairs to sit on the patio with the kids and me for about ten minutes. The kids had kept running up to her with their jars, showing her their bugs like it was gold itself.

I went upstairs and gave a quick knock on Mrs. Curtis's door. I opened it up in case she was already in the shower. Maybe she would want to drive down to the hospital with me.

She was leaning across the bed when I walked

in with my tray. She clanged her glass against the lamp as she set it down quickly.

I'm sure she saw me frown, because she looked guilty for a second, and then she looked real pleased with the way things were going. She reached over and picked up her glass again and lifted it up toward me like she was toasting me.

"Here's to the amazing Kitty Lee . . . superwoman."

She took a sip of the amber liquid and started to giggle. Her shoulders shook up and down, jiggling the glass till it spilled down the front of her nightgown.

"Have some tea, Mrs. Curtis. It's herbal."

Mrs. Curtis took another sip from her glass. "Thanks, but I prefer my own tea . . . it's made from grain, you know."

I set her tray down and turned to go. Mrs. Curtis was sliding back into her rumpled state. I had her showered and up last night, but here she was, back in bed and drinking again. Last night I had only polished up the outside.

"I'm taking the kids over to my gramma's for a picnic," I explained. "If that's all right with you."

Mrs. Curtis let her head hang back as she laughed. "Whatever, Kitty. I trust my kids with you. I trust my husband with you, too." She laughed again. "Bradley said you were a lifesaver, did you know that?"

"I'm glad to help out." I put my hand on the door. I knew I would never be able to help Mrs. Curtis. She needed to go away to one of those fancy places and get help.

"Oh, don't rush off." Mrs. Curtis pulled a shoe

box out from under her bed. She removed the lid and pulled out a small pint bottle. "Stay and have a drink with me."

"No, thanks. The kids are waiting."

Mrs. Curtis started to pour another drink, then set the bottle down hard on her nightstand. "I bet you don't drink, do you, Kitty? I bet you don't even try to get my husband alone in some dark corner, now, do you?" Mrs. Curtis studied me like she was searching for his fingerprints on me. She shrugged and gave a hard laugh. "You probably wouldn't be the first, you know. I see how women look at Brad." She sat down on the end of the bed and rolled her head against the headboard. "But you're some little churchgoer, aren't you? Brad told me the kids need someone like you right now. You must be very, very good at what you do, Kitty Lee."

I opened the door, not wanting to hear any more.

"Well, you're not. Not really," Mrs. Curtis said. "Nobody stays good in this crummy world for long. You're just young, that's all. Young and too stupid to know what life is all about."

Mrs. Curtis kicked the tray off her table with her foot. "I don't need your scraps. I don't need *you* at all."

I was halfway down the large upstairs hall when Mrs. Curtis flung open her bedroom door. She lurched forward, steadying herself on the railing.

"Just a reminder, Kitty Lee . . . you're nothing but hired help to this family. That's all you are to me, my children, and especially my husband. You're not our first baby-sitter, you know. Not by a long shot." She pointed her finger at me. "So don't let your small-town imagination run away with you. You can drag my family to a thousand hick carnivals but it won't change a thing. Don't go thinking you're anything more than summer help."

My hands started trembling so bad I shoved them deep into my jeans. I stared right back at her until she slammed her bedroom door so hard the light in the hall swayed.

I passed the den and stopped. Joey told me his daddy slept in the den a lot. The plaid afghan was laying in a crumpled heap on the end of the couch. As soon as I picked it up, I could smell the spicy soap Mr. Curtis used. I wondered how he ever ended up with that woman. He must have loved her at one time, so she must have been nicer once.

I refolded the blanket into a small neat square and laid it on the back of the couch. Mr. Curtis would know the moment he walked into the room that someone had been thinking about him. I took an empty coffee cup from the stand and walked down the wide spiral staircase, thinking of how wonderful it would be to live in such a splendid house, surrounded by such nice little kids.

Mrs. Curtis surely didn't deserve all that she had. She didn't deserve a bit of it.

Chapter Twenty

Gramma Belle was already standing in the front yard, tying up her morning glories, when the kids and I pulled up. She was wearing a big straw hat and a pair of Pop's old blue jeans. Except for her thick gray bun at the base of her neck, she looked just like a kid herself.

Gramma must have felt bad about listening to the gossip at the Tupperware party because she picked up the basket and practically pushed me out of the yard. "You go down and see how their daddy is feeling and then meet us by the bridge if you can. Wayne and Jackie called this morning to borrow a saw so I invited them to come along, too. Try to hurry, Kitty. We'll try to save you a sandwich, but we can't promise a thing about the ginger cookies, right, kids?"

Joey took the big basket and the girls each reached up a hand for Gramma's and they all started walking down the alley. It wasn't until they were at the corner that they remembered to wave.

I got back in the car and went uptown to get a funny get-well card for Mr. Curtis. I had a pocket full of homemade cards the kids had colored last night, but I wanted mine to be a little special, what with him almost losing his finger and all.

I was in aisle six of the drugstore, laughing out loud over a verse, when somebody poked me in the back. It was Cody, stabbing me with his Milky Way.

"Hey, Kitty Lee. Don't tell me you finally learned how to read."

"Funny, Cody." Actually, I'm surprised I answered him at all since I was so shocked he was speaking to me. He had acted so strange at the carnival the other night. Dottie said that Cody and Jessica had some sort of a fight at the softball game a couple of days ago. Jessica had wanted to go out for dinner in Shanks and Cody said he had been playing softball with his friends during the summer since he was ten and he sure wasn't going to stop now, and that if Jessica was so hungry, she could just go order herself shrimp in a basket and eat it till the cows came home.

Dottie said Jessica hollered right back and pretty soon the umpire had to come over and yell "Let's play ball!" right in Cody's ear.

So maybe that fight reminded Cody that none of us are perfect and he'd better forgive and forget or he wouldn't have a friend left to call his own. I missed Cody being my friend, too. I smiled and showed him the card, feeling the strain between us starting to give, like wore-out elastic finally remembering to snap back.

131

Cody glanced at the card, looking back up at me without a smile so I know he didn't read it. "So you're still baby-sitting up there? My mom said that Gramma Belle didn't like the idea anymore. Everyone in town saw you two hanging on each other at the carnival."

My cheeks blazed red, wondering if Gramma Belle had offered an opinion or two at Myrna's Tupperware party after all. Maybe those ladies with their lettuce crispers and burpable bowls just backed her into a corner and she had to say something so they would know she was taking care of me.

"Yes, I am still working for Mr. Curtis," I said in a very cool and official voice. I put the card back in the rack and pulled out another. "And I was not hanging on him at the carnival. It was a friendly hug. As a matter of fact, Mr. Curtis is in the hospital right now with a severe cut, Cody. I wish this town would extend a little sympathy."

Cody laughed so hard, I jumped. "Yeah, well tell him not to fall over his gin bottle next time and he won't get cut. Word has it that he has a serious drinking problem."

I nearly fell into the magazine rack. A drinking problem? Poor Mr. Curtis had scads of problems, but none of them were his doing.

"You're crazy, Cody. Mr. Curtis doesn't drink at all. I've been working at his house for weeks now so I suppose I should know. Last Saturday afternoon I asked him if he wanted a beer with his pizza, and he looked at me like I was out of my mind."

Cody just sort of grunted and pointed his Milky

Way right in my face. "Me thinks he does protest too much."

I swatted his candy bar away. "Me thinks you don't know what you're talking about."

Mrs. Owens was hurrying down the aisle, her ear cocked in our direction. She stopped just a yard short of us, pretending to look through the wrapping paper, but she was tilting her head toward us. Cody took my arm and pushed me back another yard or two.

"James's uncle works for sanitation and he said that more bottles come out of that house than the Moose Club. And the kid who delivers from the market said that he gets a ten-dollar tip if he delivers two bottles of whiskey along with the cornflakes."

I could have reminded him then and there that if it was Mr. Curtis's drinking problem he could have run into Fort Ashby in the dark of night to load up his car with booze. But I couldn't bring myself to spread it around. If Mr. Curtis wanted to keep his wife's problem a secret, then I would honor it till I could talk to him about it.

Mrs. Owens moved down our way, smiling and poking through the get-well cards like she needed ten or twenty.

"I can't tell you the whole story, Cody," I whispered, "but take it from me, Mr. Curtis is a nice, nice man and he doesn't drink. You tell James and your other friends to give the Curtises a chance. I've gotten real close to them over the weeks."

"Yeah, so I've heard. I heard you were real close to *him*," hissed Cody. "And don't think the whole town hasn't seen you driving around in his fancy car. Does he give you a spending allowance, too, Kitty? Kind of a bonus for all your little duties?"

Cody shoved me back, crushing me against the sympathy cards. "He's old enough to be your father, for Pete's sake!"

I shook his hand off me. "So what is *that* suppose to mean?"

"It means you better get away from that house before you do real damage to your reputation. I couldn't believe the way you two were carrying on at the carnival in front of everyone. You're in over your head, Kitty Lee."

Cody turned and left then, his arms swinging so hard he bumped Mrs. Owens's straw bag right off her arm.

"Here you go," I said as I handed it back.

"Thank you, dear." Mrs. Owens was trying hard not to grin as she watched Cody storm outside. "My, Cody seems a little upset this morning."

"Cody has been setting in the sun too long, Mrs. Owens." I grabbed a get-well card with a bunny sniffing a flower. I didn't even bother to read the verse. I just wanted to get out of here and away from Cody's words, which still hung in the air.

Mrs. Owens reached out her hand and stopped me as I walked past. "Excuse me, Kitty Lee, but I couldn't help overhearing . . . someone called me just last night and said that Mr. Curtis had cut his foot off. How is he?"

"He cut his hand, Mrs. Owens, and he's fine. I'm just on my way over to the hospital now. I'll tell him you asked about him."

Mrs. Owens's thin, penciled eyebrows shot up.

"Oh, you're going to visit him? At his hospital room?" She looked shocked like I had just announced I was going dancing with him.

"Yes! Yes, I am, Mrs. Owens!" I said a little loudly. How come I had lived in Romney for sixteen years and this was the first time I was looking at their small-time ways right in the face?

She took a step closer, lowering her voice to include only me. "And then I heard week before last that Mrs. Curtis wasn't doing too well either. The garden club has sent her at least two invitations to tea since they moved into that lovely big house, and Mr. Curtis declined both, saying his wife was feeling poorly. Is that true, Kitty? Is Mrs. Curtis really too ill to attend our August meeting? We always have such a nice time and this August we are paying a man to drive up from Cumberland to show slides of the great gardens of — "

"She is fine, Mrs. Owens," I cut in quick, starting to walk backward to the cash register. "Her nerves are a bit ragged, is all. Understandable with the move from New York and all."

"Yes, of course."

"But she is feeling better every day," I added, not wanting any more rumors to go flying around town. The Curtis kids didn't need to start school in September with tales about their mother meeting them at the door.

Mrs. Owens put back her card and followed me up the aisle. "Maybe I should drop by this afternoon with a sweet potato casserole, no . . . maybe my chicken with biscuit top, or I could always make a meat loaf or . . ."

"Thank you for thinking of them, but to tell you

135

the truth, we have food coming out of our eyes at the house. I made a big pot of chili this morning, and the kids said they wanted hot dogs on the grill for supper. As soon as I get back from the hospital, the kids and I are making a welcome home chocolate cake for Mr. Curtis." I was talking a mile a minute. "I'm sure Mr. Curtis and his wife will be welcoming folks into their new home real soon, once things calm down some."

That seemed to perk Mrs. Owens up a bit. Her dialing fingers were practically twitching.

I paid for the card and pushed open the door. The sunlight hit me full face, so I bent down and fished in my pocket for the car keys. It wasn't until I looked up that I noticed Cody leaning against the white Mercedes. His arms were crossed and he had his eyes closed, his face lifted up to the sun. If I didn't know how mean he was, his good looks would have stopped me all over again. It startled me, seeing him looking so tall and muscular. Made him seem more of a stranger than his new sudden bouts of meanness.

"Excuse me," I said, jingling the keys and waiting for him to move.

Cody lowered his head and looked me straight in the eye. I could smell his spearmint gum as he leaned forward and gave me a real nice smile. "Something I can do for you, Kitty Lee?"

"I want to get into my car."

He laughed and stepped aside. "Oh yeah, yeah. For a second there, I forgot that this is *your* car now. James said he saw you driving home from the carnival in it. I was used to you driving your

pop's old Chevy. But that was back in B.C. time
. . ." Cody laughed. "Before Curtis."

I put my hand on the handle, sighing and knowing Cody was getting ready to give me a hard time
again.

"So what does Mrs. Curtis think about you and
her husband? Or do you try not to hold hands in
front of the wife or the kids?" Cody leaned his
angry face closer to mine. "What is it you two do,
exactly?"

The car keys dropped right out of my hand.
When I bent down to pick up the keys, tears fell
right out of me. I stayed down long enough to
wipe them off best I could.

"You've got a dirty mind, Cody."

He just laughed deep in his throat. He kept
watching my face but even when he saw the tears
welling up again, he didn't care. He just went on
being as cruel as he knew how to be.

"Quite a summer for you, Kitty Lee. You've
come a far piece from the Dairy Queen, that's for
sure. Don't think people aren't talking either."

Cody yanked open my car door. "Your coach
awaits you, my dear."

I got in and put the key in. The air conditioner
and radio both roared on, music blasting. I
snapped them off and pushed the gear into re-
verse, hoping Cody wouldn't see that my hand
was shaking.

Cody leaned down, sticking his face inside the
window.

"Yeah, pretty fancy trappings, all right." Cody
tapped his class ring against the car's window.

"Well . . . enjoy it, Kitty Lee. I'm sure you've earned it."

Cody slammed his fist down on the hood of the car as he walked away. So he didn't see me start to cry. He didn't turn around once to see how I looked with a broken heart.

Chapter Twenty-one

As soon as I turned the corner from the drugstore, I let the tears fall. Cody had to be the meanest person in the whole world. I had to talk to Dottie fast and find out if what Cody had been saying was true, if people really were talking about me and Mr. Curtis. Maybe Dottie could help me understand what changed Cody so this summer. Anyone could tell that the outside of him had changed, what with the four inches and all those muscles. Male hormones must have struck through him like an electrical storm, leaving him a changed person. I turned the radio back on, missing the old Cody, the Cody that would have socked anyone right in the nose for talking like he just did to me. Seemed a dead fact that all those muscles had eaten every last bit of sensibility away.

Shoot, if I were to believe Cody, people were in their kitchens right now, sipping coffee and discussing me and Mr. Curtis. Not a lick of what he said was true. Mr. Curtis was a gentleman. That little, harmless kiss on my hand in the hospital was probably related to all the drugs they were dripping into him to ease the pain.

I was so busy talking out loud to myself that I almost drove past Dottie's house. I slowed down, tooting twice before pulling into the driveway. Dottie and her mother were hanging clothes out in the side yard.

"Well, Kitty Lee Carter, just look at you," laughed Dottie's mom. She dropped her clothespins and walked right over, running her hand down the hood of the car. "Isn't this a pretty car? Don't tell me Gramma Belle finally went and won something big at Bingo."

"I wish. It belongs to Mr. Curtis." I left the door open when I got out so she could peek inside without looking too nosy.

"Air-conditioning, C.D. player, even a car phone" — Mrs. Ramsey slid behind the wheel — "I sure could get used to this in a hurry. Does Mr. Curtis let you drive it whenever you want?"

"No. I just have it today since he's in the hospital."

Mrs. Ramsey looked real interested, then confused. She got out of the car and closed the door. "Now, Dottie, why didn't you tell me any of this? I asked you what was new with Kitty Lee and you said, 'Nothing.' "

Dottie shot me a panic-stricken look. We never did get a chance to talk yet about where she spent the night last night.

"Well, Kitty asked me not to say anything . . ." Dottie looked at me hopefully.

"Until we knew how he was doing," I said hurriedly. "He cut his hand and he almost lost his finger. But he's doing fine now."

Mrs. Ramsey grinned. "I can't believe you were planning to keep this good story to yourself, Dottie. You knew I was going to have my hair colored this afternoon. You can't expect me to go into Thelma's empty-handed."

"Kitty and I talked about so many things last night. I guess the business about Mr. Curtis cutting his foot . . ."

"Hand," I corrected.

"Slipped my mind. Come on up on the porch, Kitty. I'll fix us all some iced tea."

As I followed Dottie up the walk, I felt like pinching her hard. Where in the world *did* she spend the night last night? Glory Ned anyway. First Cody and now Dottie, both of them changing their colors like a couple of chameleons. Wasn't anybody going to make it through the summer without changing?

"Gramma Belle says to say a special hello to you and Ludy," added Dottie, turning to smile at her mother like she was speaking the gospel's truth.

Mrs. Ramsey checked her watch. "I'd better dash or I'll be late." She ran her fingers through her curly red hair, making a face like she must look plain awful, which she never did.

Dottie brought out the iced tea and we both watched her mother back out the drive and head up the road.

"I tried calling you from Fort Ashby," Dottie started explaining as soon as her mother turned the bend. "But your dad said you weren't coming in till late, and then Gramma Belle said you weren't coming in at all so I just pretended to be somebody else and hung up." Dottie kept stirring her tea, looking at it instead of me. "So then, Ronnie said that we could both just stay with friends of his."

I set down my tea without saying a word. The whole time she was talking, I just stared a hole right through her. I knew what she was saying. She was practically standing up on a tree stump and shouting that she went and slept with a boy.

"I don't believe you really spent the night with him!" As soon as the words came out, I knew it was Gramma's voice I was using.

Dottie sighed, setting her tea down next to mine. "I love him, Kitty Lee. It makes a difference; it makes a real big difference."

I gave her my best, stupid, "Gee, how can I possibly understand all this mature stuff?" look.

Dottie sighed and moved away from me on the swing. I knew I was ruining her big news about Ronnie loving her. I guess I should have kept up my subscriptions to the teen magazines so I could read articles like, "What to Say When Your Best Friend Tells You She Slept with a Boy!" Those magazine people might even give you three or four things to say so you could vary your response from time to time.

But all I said was, "Shoot, Dottie!"

Dottie sat there in the swing, trying to look comfortable with the silence that stood tall as an oak between us.

"You're going to end up just like Erleen Wilkes," I said, which was pure mean since Erleen had her first baby when she was fourteen and a half and has had one every spring since.

"I am not going to end up like Erleen! Honestly, Kitty, why can't you just be happy for me? Nobody has ever cared for me like Ronnie. He tells me all the time how pretty I am . . ."

"Well, you are, Dottie. But you don't spend the night in Fort Ashby with every guy who tells you so."

Dottie stood up from the swing. "Well, believe it or not, Ronnie was the first one to ever tell me, Kitty Lee. You've always had boys liking you, Kenny Hammond, Cody, Mark . . ."

I just shook my head to that.

"I thought you would understand. You're my best friend."

I laughed, this whole day had been so terrible. "Well, it's been three or four weeks and I still haven't met the guy, Dottie, so don't expect me to care a bit about him."

Dottie sat down on the swing again, tears making her eyes all shiny. My eyes started to smart, too, thinking about the things I had stopped telling Dottie. I didn't even think to call her up and tell about the kiss on the hand in the hospital, or the time Mr. Curtis came up to me in the kitchen and let his hand stay on my shoulder for such a long time that I almost expected smoke to rise up.

There seemed to be a part of our friendship that

shifted into the shade then, a cooler and not quite so bright and open place.

"Listen," I said, beginning to feel guilty about moralizing so much. "Why don't you bring Ronnie down to the dance tonight? I can't wait to meet him."

Dottie smiled then, reaching across and hugging me tight.

I told her I better get to the hospital and back before Gramma was worn to a frazzle with all those kids. I was about to tell her how mean Cody had been to me this afternoon, but Dottie started talking about Ronnie's plans for wrapping wire around the lilac bushes to make them look like something they weren't meant to look like in the first place and I never got to tell her.

I studied Dottie in the rearview mirror as I drove off. She waved, lifting her heavy blonde hair with the other hand and letting it fall back down to her waist. She looked so pretty and happy, exactly the same old Dottie I had loved for years. Seeing her like that didn't give me a clue as to how different she had become on the inside.

Thinking back, Dottie should have given me a warning. She should have found some way to let me know that this would be the last time I would ever see her standing there in her front yard, waving and acting like we had the rest of our lives together.

Chapter Twenty-two

I drove past the hospital twice, trying to ignore the voice inside nagging me to just keep on driving. Of course I should stop and see Mr. Curtis. He needed a friend right now. It was only Cody mixing me up with his dirty mind, filling my head with doubts, so I turned on my blinker and pulled into the parking lot. As I locked the car door, I swore that the next time I saw Cody I would march up and slap his face for saying what he did. No telling *what* he was busy telling his friends about me right this very minute. Why had he bothered to save my life if he was going to make it so miserable eleven years later?

Dr. Misage was coming out of Mr. Curtis's room as I was walking in. He checked his clipboard and announced that Mr. Curtis didn't need his I.V. treatment anymore and he could go home tomorrow at noon.

I broke into a huge grin. Boy, the kids would

be thrilled to death when I told them. I pushed open the heavy oak door.

"Hey, Mr. Curtis. I hear you're getting out of here tomorrow," I said cheerfully. "That sure is good news."

Mr. Curtis was sitting up in his bed, holding a newspaper with his good hand. "Hello, Kitty Lee. I didn't expect to see you. Are the children okay?"

"Sure. I just thought you might like a little company is all." I blushed beet-red as Mr. Curtis put his paper down and smiled at me like I was a lit-up birthday cake.

I pulled up a chair and told him everything the kids had said and done in the last day. "Gramma Belle says she just loves having little ones around again. I wouldn't be a bit surprised if she refused to give them back." I pulled the cards the kids had made for him out of my pocket and tried to smooth them out so they would stand up on his table.

"Thanks." He looked at me and smiled. "It's awfully nice of you to come and visit me, Kitty." Mr. Curtis reached out and squeezed my hand. I gave him a squeeze back, to be polite. Then I turned and poured him a big glass of water from his nightstand. I shifted from foot to foot, feeling a little funny all of a sudden about being alone with him. I pulled out a box of candy from my purse. "Hey, here's a little treat from the kids and me."

He looked up at me, kind of startled. I guess it sounded funny me saying, "the kids and me," like we were his little family. Mr. Curtis unwrapped the candy and offered me one.

146

"You're a very thoughtful person, Kitty."

"Thank you." Then a heavy silence moved in and after five minutes, it didn't seem like it was going to budge.

Finally, Mr. Curtis sipped some of his water and asked me about his wife. "Has Mrs. Curtis left her room since I've been in here?"

I cleared my throat, wondering how much I should sugarcoat and how much truth he could take. "Well, Mr. Curtis. Your wife did get up and take a shower. Then she came outside with us while the kids chased lightning bugs . . ."

"She did?" He sat up, looking so surprised and happy, you'd think I had just told him she had flown out the bedroom window and back. My heart just ached for Mr. Curtis. All he wanted was a normal wife. It broke my heart to see him lighting up like the Fourth of July as soon as I hinted his wife could be heading in that direction. Poor man deserved better than what he had, that was for sure. I decided then that I'd better not make her sound too good. I mean, she still spent most of her day in her dark bedroom.

"Did she eat anything?" Mr. Curtis's face went a little red with that question. He probably had some sort of a mental checklist to determine how bad off his wife was on a given day. If she's up, give her a point. If she showers, give her two points. If she makes a sandwich, add fifteen points. If she sits in her bed all morning, spilling whiskey down her nightgown, take a point away.

"Well, she didn't eat before we left, but . . ." Right away his face started to fall. "But, I'd bet she came down afterward for some . . . some . . . toast."

Mr. Curtis wasn't buying any of it. He covered his eyes with his left hand, pushing himself back against the pillows. Glory, I thought, Mr. Curtis is going to start bawling right in front of me! Oh, shoot, oh glory, glory! Why couldn't I have just *lied* and said she ate something? Mr. Curtis was draining himself dry with worry over that woman and his little kids. He was slumped over, his hand trembling as it lay across his eyes.

"You shouldn't let yourself get upset right now, Mr. Curtis," I said quietly. "Your wife is okay. The kids are fine."

I took a step closer, wondering if I should buzz for the nurse. Pain was pain, it was probably short-circuiting all through Mr. Curtis's body right now.

Mr. Curtis sat up, rubbing his eyes real fast like he was trying to wake up quick. "I hope you realize . . . it's not her fault, Kitty. Her nerves have been bad ever since she . . ." Mr. Curtis swallowed hard. "*We* lost a baby two years ago. Then last year, her father died of cancer. It's just been too much for her to handle."

I patted his arm. No wonder the family had such a hard time acting like one with so much going on.

"I try to excuse as much as I can," continued Mr. Curtis. "Our doctor prescribed mild tranquilizers, but they upset her stomach so a friend suggested wine in the afternoon, another friend said she should just relax with me and have a drink before dinner." Mr. Curtis stared out the window like his whole sorry story was flashing before his eyes. "It didn't take long for her to realize the numbness took over a lot faster if she skipped the lunch and dinner."

I took my hand from Mr. Curtis's arm and glanced at the door. As much as I cared for Mr. Curtis and his kids, I felt funny about listening to such private facts about Mrs. Curtis. And besides, I didn't like Mrs. Curtis. I tried to fight against it, but I didn't care for her at all. I know it must be a terrible heartbreak to lose a baby, but that doesn't mean you crawl back inside yourself and forget about the three little babies you already have.

"A lot of her problem is my fault," Mr. Curtis admitted.

"Why, Mr. Curtis, that just isn't true. None of it is!"

Mr. Curtis shook his head. "I was away weeks at a time last year."

"But that was your job, Mr. Curtis. It wasn't like you were just off on some fancy golf course. And you're real good with your kids."

Mr. Curtis sighed. "It's the kids I worry about most of all. Kids need a mother."

I slumped down in my chair, feeling so terribly sad myself, as if I could almost feel some sort of chain being wrapped around my heart. If my mother hadn't been killed, would she have protected me, no matter what? And now Joey and the girls were watching their mom drift farther and farther away. She was still alive, but dead for them.

"If you're so worried, you should get her some help, Mr. Curtis," I said finally. I felt like a sheriff serving a summons.

He shook his head. "You think I haven't tried, Kitty? Hell, being cooped up in her room for so long has made her lose touch with reality. Every time I mention going for help, Elaine swears she will kill herself."

Kill herself? How could a mother who loves her kids ever choose death over living, no matter how hard the living is? No mother would do that. I shivered then, and before I knew it, I was shaking like someone had just dumped a bucket of ice water down my back. How could any mother ever walk away from her baby? I felt numb, my head spinning. I hardly knew what I was thinking, right then. I mean, I knew Mrs. Curtis wasn't a *good* mother, facts were facts. Any woman who would shut herself away from her children. . . . A hot wave of nausea washed over me. Images of cribs and wicker baskets and diapers and . . . and Momma. And of Momma shutting herself away from me. Is that what happened? Did Momma shut herself away from Pop, from me, months before she tore down the highway? Was she running away from us, or to something better? Why else would Pop and Gramma Belle refuse to talk about that night? Thinking back, all I could piece together was hearing how Momma wasn't feeling well before her car accident; how Momma hired a girl from town to help with me so she could rest more; how Momma spent a lot of time in bed. I drew my hand up and wiped away the hot, stinging tears. The truth was bearing down on me like someone had just let it out of a dark hole. Momma must have been leaving Pop and me that night she got killed. That's why no one talked about it. All these years I wanted to believe that Pop, Momma, and me had been so happy together. It hadn't been that way at all. Momma must have closed her door on Pop and me long before she had been killed in the accident. Momma had drifted off just like Mrs. Curtis. Drifted far, far away, and then allowed a truck to snap the line forever.

"Kitty?" Mr. Curtis reached out and put his hand on my shoulder. "Honey, are you all right?" Mr. Curtis flung back his white sheet and got out of bed.

I shook my head, feeling it hang heavy on my neck. I felt his warm hand, digging into my shoulder. The bad feeling about Momma was a part of me now, a cross I felt I had to bear without a whimper, since I had been so dumb and had taken so long to figure it out. Once you knew the truth, it was impossible to move away from it. No wonder Pop was driving himself crazy. Maybe he had figured things out too late himself. Pop probably kicked himself every day wondering if he could have helped Momma find the will to live. Had he been too hard on her? Had he shouted for her to get up and take care of the baby . . . to take care of *me*? I slumped forward and leaned against Mr. Curtis. He felt so strong. *He* was trying so hard to take care of *his* kids.

Maybe Pop just didn't know how to make sense of it for Momma. All the daily chores that spin round and round like the spokes of a wheel, maybe they ran over her and crushed her. Momma got in the car that night to end it all.

"Kitty?" Mr. Curtis rubbed my back with his good hand. "Tell me what's wrong."

I felt like a dime-store rubber doll. My heart was so numb, I barely felt Mr. Curtis wrap his arms around me. I saw his face draw closer, felt his whiskered cheek against mine, but I felt nothing, like it was all happening to some girl on the movie screen down at the Regent.

"Are you okay?" he whispered. His voice was low, unsure, like he was asking us both the same question. "Am I making you sad?"

I started crying then, big, gulping sounds coming from a place so deep in me, I didn't know it existed.

"I'm okay." I *wasn't*, but I had to drop anchor. A current was starting to drag me downstream.

Mr. Curtis looked into my eyes. He seemed sad, too. "Maybe I should have left you down at Jake's, after all."

"Maybe," I said slowly. Part of me was glad he didn't. Part of me wanted to hate him for taking me away from the safety of where I had been. But it was too late to wonder about all that. It was too late to go back to being the same exact Kitty Lee I had been. So when Mr. Curtis bent down to kiss me, I kissed him back.

Chapter Twenty-three

I'd never kissed anyone like that before. Up till then, I'd only kissed boys in someone's gameroom, with records blaring and someone's mom ready to come down the stairs with a tray of chip n' dip. When I kissed Mr. Curtis I could almost feel my toes melt. Mr. Curtis kissed me again, pulling me against him. He scared me then, acting so hungry. I felt liable to disappear in the smoke of that kiss! I jerked back.

"We shouldn't be doing this, Mr. Curtis!" I said. I pushed him away.

Mr. Curtis followed me to the window. "Kitty, I thought you felt the same way I did," he said at last.

"But . . . but, I don't know how you feel at all!" I felt the tears stinging. I was lying. I did know how he felt because part of me felt the same way back. Mr. Curtis was such a nice man. I did like him. I liked him a lot. It scared me to think of how many times I thought about Mr. Curtis calling me honey, or putting his arms around me to give me a hug. I knew he was a married man, but lately, in my dreams, he was just Mr. Curtis, a man who didn't really belong to anyone except me and the kids. And yet. . . .

"We can't kiss each other anymore, Mr. Curtis. Not ever again."

Mr. Curtis looked at me for a long time. Even now I don't know if he was trying to decide something, or if he was just dumbfounded. "Don't you care about me, Kitty?"

"Of course," I said softly. "I think you're one of the nicest men I've ever met. You're so kind and nice to the kids." I drew in a deep breath and turned to face him. "You're so good to me, Mr. Curtis. I like you a lot, and I don't think it's right. It's getting too easy to forget you're a married man."

Mr. Curtis laughed. "You call what I have a marriage?"

"Yes," I said softly. It was a troubled marriage, but it *was* a marriage.

"Our house is finally happy with you there, Kitty." Mr. Curtis stood up and smoothed back his hair. "I respect your feelings, Kitty. I promise I won't touch you again." He gave me a lopsided grin and held up his good hand. "Scout's honor."

Mr. Curtis looked so young and handsome standing there. And I knew he would try his hardest to keep his promise. We would have both tried. But Gramma Belle told me a thousand times that even the most careful get burned if they walk into a burning building. And Mr. Curtis wanted me in his life so bad right then that I could feel the heat. And I felt the same way.

"I'm sorry, Mr. Curtis, but I just can't work at your house once you come home. I'll ask if Gramma Belle can watch the kids for the rest of the summer. She loves your — "

"Kitty, don't do this." Mr. Curtis reached out and touched my arm, then took it back fast. His blue eyes were so troubled. "Don't do this, Kitty. We aren't doing anything wrong."

I just looked at him, sad with knowing that if I came back, we might.

"I have to go back to Jake's. It will be better for everyone." My decision was already breaking my heart. How stupid to think I could play house. What rules were there for that?

"I'll talk to Gramma Belle when I get home," I said quietly.

Mr. Curtis just turned and stared out the window, shaking his head like I was making a big mistake. I picked up the car keys and walked out of the hospital room. As I walked across the parking lot, I could feel Mr. Curtis's eyes on me. I didn't look up. I couldn't look up. If he had waved me back right then, I might have gone.

Chapter Twenty-four

Gramma Belle suspected something was wrong right off the bat. She hurried out the back door with a dish towel slung over her shoulder and all but circled me, sniffing for clues like a hound dog.

"Nothing is *wrong*, Gramma," I lied. Everything was wrong. "I told Mr. Curtis I wanted to go back to Jake's and he wondered if you could help him out. Come on kids, time to get home and cleaned up. Your daddy is coming home tomorrow."

The kids smiled about that, but they still wanted to play. Waiting isn't part of a kid's day.

"Can we go to your cousins' clubhouse *before* we go home?" Joey wanted to know. "I've been real helpful all day, right, Gramma Belle? I swept the porch and helped pick a bushel of corn."

Janice held up a plastic bag filled with cookies. "We made these today, Kitty. I got to break all the eggs."

"Can't we *please* go to the clubhouse, Kitty?" Joey asked again.

"No, let's just get back," I said shortly. My head was about to split in two.

Gramma sat down heavy in the lawn chair and picked up the apple she had been peeling. She squinted across the yard at me. "What's eating you anyway?"

"Nothing!" I said for the tenth time. I looked down at my shoes, still feeling her eyes boring a hole straight through me so the facts would come pouring out.

"Oh, all right," I sighed. "But we're only staying a minute, you hear?"

"Yippee!" cried Chrissy. She ran over and leaned her elbows on Gramma's lap. "You come, too, okay?"

Gramma laughed. "Mercy, no. I'd fall on my head for sure."

We all laughed then. Glancing over at the house, I noticed Pop's bedroom window shade was pulled. "Did Pop come home early today?"

Gramma shook her head. She chewed on her bottom lip a minute before she looked back up at me. "No, Kitty. Honey, today he just never went into work, is all." Gramma's mouth grew taut. She tossed another apple slice into the pan and looked out at the back line where her wash hung.

My heart slid right down into my shoes. What was wrong with people anymore? Every time I turned around someone was mad at life, drinking to forget it, or just *hiding* from it behind a closed bedroom door. What was so all fired wrong with living that made people turn their back on it?

My chest hurt, wondering why Momma had to be one of them, wondering if Pop was going to drive himself crazy wondering if he had done all the wrong things.

I gathered up the kids, tramping through the house as loudly as I could. "Wake up, Pop!" each step seemed to shout. "Wake up and see what you're doing."

Chrissy looked up at me, and I could tell she was curious about all this noise, noise that wasn't allowed at her own house. But I just smiled back at her and then Joey and Janice joined hands and started stomping around the porch swing. I started to smile as I led them off the porch. By the time we got to the bottom step, Gramma Belle was standing in the yard with her hands on her hips. I could see she was wondering about all the noise we had been making.

"Say good-bye to Gramma Belle," I whispered quickly.

" 'Bye, Gramma Belle," they called.

"I love you, Gramma!" shouted Chrissy in her high, clear voice.

I turned to wave as we loaded into the car. Gramma raised her hand and waved back. But through the rearview mirror I could see she was worried. I shoved the mirror up with my hand as I backed out.

"I sure like living in Romney," Joey said from the backseat. "At first I hated it, but I like it now."

"You'll like it even more once school starts," I said. "Wayne will be in your grade come September."

Janice cut in. "And Gramma Belle said they

have dancing school right near my house. I'll get shiny black shoes that make a lot of noise on the kitchen floor."

Soon they were all talking at once, about the dog they might get and the basketball hoop that would look great in the back driveway. By the time I parked the car and we had walked to the clubhouse, it was already the hottest part of the afternoon. No one was around, so we climbed right up. I stood behind Chrissy with my hand on her little rear end so she wouldn't fall off the ladder.

"Holy cow," I said as soon as I reached the top. "I haven't been up here in at least four years. I remember thinking this clubhouse was as tall as the Sears building and now I can hardly stand up here!"

"Isn't this great?" asked Joey. He leaned against the back of the tree and looked out across the field. "This is the best tree house in the whole world. I can't wait till ours is finished."

"Let's have a cookie," suggested Janice. She sat down and unwrapped the bag. We all reached for a cookie.

"We can save Wayne and Jackie cookies, too," Janice said. "I'll hide them right here in this hole."

"I hope they come soon," said Joey, bending down a branch and scanning the backyard.

I took another bite of cookie, and thought about leaving right then. I didn't mind if the little boys came down from the house. But I sure didn't want to see Cody right now. He would take one look at me and know Mr. Curtis had kissed me. I just knew it.

"Can we bring Daddy here?" asked Janice.

"And Mommy?" added Chrissy. "We can carry her."

Before I could even answer, Joey did. "Not Mom, just Dad."

The cookie inside my mouth suddenly felt heavy, like I was sucking on a stone. Joey was barely eight years old and he was instructing his little sisters in how to cut their momma out of their lives. Lives that had just gotten started.

"Well, hey now, Joey. I'd bet your momma would like being out here with all the pretty trees." I kept my voice real light so they wouldn't realize I was trying to tell them what to do. "It would be nice for her being so close to the blue sky."

Joey and Janice just shrugged. Chrissy was too busy trying to pick up a fuzzy caterpillar.

"Mommy doesn't come out of her room much," explained Janice slowly, thinking maybe I hadn't noticed before.

"She just stays in her room so she doesn't have to take care of us," added Joey. He sounded more mad than sad.

Janice leaned against me. "I'm glad *you* take good care of us, Kitty Lee. I wish you could start being our mommy."

Chrissy laughed and held up two fingers. "Two mommies."

Joey looked down at me, a hopeful look in his eyes. I had to turn away then, rubbing at my eyes like the wind had just blown something in. I kept my head turned away, too ashamed to even look at those kids. I hadn't deliberately set out to steal love in their family, love that rightly belonged to their momma. Even though she seemed to be pushing it away with both hands, the love was rightly hers.

I took a deep breath and turned back. I took Joey's and Janice's hand and squeezed them. "I love being your baby-sitter. But I could never be your mommy. You already have a momma. And even though she isn't too much fun now, since she doesn't feel good, she will get better soon."

"No, she won't," Joey said. His voice was as flat as a nickel. "Don't you like my dad?"

"Of course I do."

"Daddy likes you," said Janice. "He said if I drink all my milk I'll grow up pretty like you."

"I'm going to talk to your daddy. You know how special Romney is. Maybe there is a special doctor here that could make your mom feel better."

Janice smiled. "Maybe give her a shot."

Joey squeezed my hand. "I have lots of money in my bank. We could buy her two shots and she would get better even faster."

I reached out and hugged them all. They still loved their momma. There was still time to get her out of bed and downstairs where she belonged.

Gramma Belle always says that I take the cake for offering first and checking to see if it's possible second. But sometimes you've got to jump in while the boat's in sight and swim to it, or you'll be left on the dock standing still. Those kids needed a momma, and judging from the kiss Mr. Curtis gave me in the hospital, he needed his wife back.

I stood up and stretched, reaching both hands up to the sky. The breeze zigzagged its way through the branches of the oaks and lifted our hair right up by the roots.

"Whew!" I cried, "Isn't this the best fun?"

As the wind finally blew over the hill, I heard rustling and twigs snapping like firecrackers below us.

I stuck my head under the railing. All I could see was the back of Cody's head as he disappeared through the thick patch of honeysuckle growing near the clubhouse.

Chapter Twenty-five

"Cody!" I yelled. I didn't expect him to answer. I watched the tail end of his shirt disappear up the hill. That sneaky old Cody had turned into a regular spy. No telling *how* long he had been crouched in the honeysuckle, just waiting to grab himself some more tales to carry around town about me.

"Kids, let's get back to the house," I said, heading down the ladder first and helping Chrissy. "Your daddy is going to be coming home tomorrow and we want to get things ready for him."

"Mr. Bear is at Gramma's," Chrissy said. "Let's go get him fast."

As soon as we walked into the kitchen, the phone was ringing. "Hi," said Dottie. "Ronnie finished his job sculpting down at the shoe factory today. Everyone got a fifty-dollar bonus for doing such a fast job."

"Great. Can you both go to the dance tonight?"

"Of course. We'll pick you up around seven-thirty." I was glad to hear that Dottie actually wanted me to meet Ronnie.

Gramma Belle said she would baby-sit the Curtis kids, if they were all set for bed when she got there.

The rest of the afternoon flew by. I took the kids back to their house, shampooed and fed the whole bunch of them.

By six o'clock I had them in front of the television watching Walt Disney, each with their own little dish of corn curls. As I cleaned up the kitchen, I could hear them laughing. It was so easy to turn an evening with kids into a party. Mrs. Curtis sure was missing a lot of good times. I dove my hands into the soapy water, not wanting to even start thinking about my own momma. I refused to think about it anymore till I was able to talk to Pop about what had really happened. Now that I knew this much, I had to know the whole story or I'd start inventing things.

I turned on the dishwasher and went up the back staircase to check on Mrs. Curtis. I hadn't spoken to her since she had been so insulting to me.

"Evening, Mrs. Curtis," I said. Mrs. Curtis didn't even jump anymore when I burst through her door. I had been bothering her on such a regular basis, that she almost expected it. "Gramma Belle sent over some split pea soup and I was wondering if you wanted some."

"No, thank you."

"Mr. Curtis will be getting out of the hospital tomorrow." I walked over and smoothed out the blankets like I thought she was truly ill. "I'm going out a little later so my Gramma Belle will be by to watch the kids. Give a holler if you need anything."

I figured Mr. Curtis could explain why Gramma Belle would be taking my place from now on.

Mrs. Curtis raised one eyebrow. "Yes, I'll be sure to . . . *holler*."

I just let that roll right off me. Between Cody and Mrs. Curtis hurling insulting words at me, I was building up a thick layer of protective oil on my emotions.

As I passed the mirrored closet, I slid the door shut. It bumped against a shoe box sticking out.

"Don't mind that," Mrs. Curtis said quickly, half rising from her bed.

Reaching down, I pushed it back in. The lid flew up and a pint-size bottle of whiskey lay nestled in the hot-pink tissue paper.

"Let me just tidy up some," I said as I grabbed the bottle. "The children are downstairs watching television if you want to come down and say good night." I mentioned her children every chance I got so she would remember they were right below her. I would remind Gramma Belle to have the kids tiptoe in to say good night, too, even if Mrs. Curtis was pretending to be asleep. The other day I set a huge jar of peppermints by Mrs. Curtis's lamp. I told her she might want to offer one to the kids when they came in to say hello. But by the way she studied me, I think she knew I was telling her to pop one in her mouth after she finished drinking her liquor so the kids couldn't smell it on her.

165

"Mrs. Curtis?" I waited till she looked up at me. "There's probably a good specialist down at the hospital. Maybe you could go talk to him."

Mrs. Curtis drew herself up, and a tremor of fear flashed in her eyes. "No. I'll be fine. I just . . . just need to rest."

I sat down on the end of her bed. "If you were any more rested, you'd be dead."

We both looked at each other for a long time. I don't know why I said what I did, next. Maybe to scare her. Maybe to let her know how lucky she was. "My momma is already dead. I didn't have much of a choice in not having a momma. That's why I can't understand you not trying to get better. You're not giving your kids a choice, either."

I got up and walked out then 'cause I knew Mrs. Curtis wasn't going to be saying anything back. She still had the shovel in her hand, digging a moat around herself so nobody could touch her.

Gramma Belle was already sitting in the easy chair with Chrissy when I came downstairs.

"I came early so you could run home and take a shower and get pretty," laughed Gramma. "Go on now, we'll be fine."

I promised to tell them all about the dance tomorrow. Gramma would baby-sit tonight and had hired someone from the church to stay overnight.

The summer air felt good as I walked home. The idea of going to a dance was exciting. I had been so busy at the Curtises', I hadn't even seen any of the kids from school in weeks. Tonight would probably be the last big dance before school so everyone would be there. The Christian Women's League of Romney rented the second floor of the Byrnes & Kiefer Bakery Supply Warehouse on Rosemary Lane for the summer dances. Not only was it big enough, but on hot summer nights, the smell of cinnamon and chocolate drifted up through the floorboards.

I sat down in the porch swing for a few minutes, listening to the silence in the house. I considered going inside and banging on Pop's door to ask him a few questions. Wake up, Pop. Tell me about Momma. How long was she shut up in her room? Did she drink whiskey out of a coffee cup? Did she tear out of the house and get into the car that night because she was angry?

I kicked off my shoes and walked my toes back and forth against the smooth gray floor. Maybe I didn't want to know. What if I sewed together the bits and pieces of what Pop told me and ended up with Momma being just as unloving as Mrs. Curtis? A woman who would rather lie in bed to avoid any more pain, instead of looking beyond it for the good.

I heard the clock chiming inside so I got off the swing. Tomorrow would be soon enough to look for more answers. Tonight I was going to go to the dance and get together with my friends. If only for a night I was going to get as far away from troubles as I could. After I washed my hair, put on a new summer dress to show off my tan, and painted my nails Flamingo Pink, I was going to have some fun.

Chapter Twenty-six

I was twirling around the living room, singing with the radio when Dottie popped her head in the door. "Practicing for the big dance?"

Dottie looked positively radiant. She was wearing a new green dress with a green and hot pink scarf tying back her hair. "Let me look at you!" I walked around her like I was about to award a blue ribbon.

"Ronnie bought this scarf for me with his bonus!"

I could tell Dottie felt as pretty as she looked. She walked around the living room, touching the back of Gramma's rocker, straightening my school picture in the walnut frame. When she picked up the tiny china angel she had given me back in the third grade, she started laughing.

"I still can't believe you keep this thing in your living room."

"Of course I do. Your mother made you dig up

a hundred dandelions out of your yard before she would buy it." I took the angel back from her and kissed it before I set it back on the mantle. "And you made me buy you one for your birthday four months later."

Dottie smiled, then frowned. "Yeah, well, mine got broken in one of my parents' more interesting fights." She stared wistfully at the angel. Something inside me insisted that I go ahead and give it to her.

"Here, Dottie. Let's share April angel, then. You keep it six months, and then give it back to me."

Dottie rolled her eyes. "No, don't be silly. It's yours."

"It's ours," I said.

Dottie took the angel, holding it gently in her hand as if it were a baby bird. She grew awfully serious and put her hand on my shoulder like she was about to go into battle. "Don't ever forget you're my best friend, Kitty Lee. My very *best* . . ."

I knew one of us had to do something to lighten things up or we'd both be bawling. So I pulled her pretty silk scarf down on her eyes. "Where is Ronnie?"

Dottie pushed her scarf up and linked one arm with mine. "Oh, I can hardly wait for the two people I love the most in the whole world to finally meet." Dottie stopped just short of the screen door. She lowered her voice so I had to bend down to hear. "I think that's why I delayed this meeting so long, Kitty. I was just so afraid you two might not like each other and then what would I do?"

She smiled and all but pulled me out on the

porch. Ronnie was leaning against the porch pillar, all six feet of him with red curly hair sticking out from beneath a New York Mets baseball cap.

He reached out a lanky, freckled arm and shook my hand. Then he laughed and yanked off his hat and shook my hand again. "Hi, Kitty Lee. I'm Ronnie O'Brien."

"Hi, Ronnie. Glad we're finally getting a chance to meet."

He smiled, pointing his cap at Dottie. "I kept asking Dottie to get us all together, but she was all scared that . . ."

Dottie blushed red and walked over and hugged him. "Be quiet and get us to the dance."

Ronnie held the car door open for both of us. Dottie scooted in first, smiling across her shoulder at me.

"I have heard so many stories about you, Kitty, that I feel like you're my kid sister," said Ronnie. He had a real slow way of talking that made everything he said sound so sincere and nice. I liked that till I realized this was part of the magic he had probably used on Dottie. It was that same slow voice he had probably used to convince her that it would be too inconvenient to wake Gramma Belle when there was a perfectly good bed in Fort Ashby for her.

Dottie kept her hand on Ronnie's knee and her eyes glued to his face the whole trip over to Rosemary Lane. To be perfectly honest, I had already planned on disliking Ronnie. First of all, for talking her into staying with him in Fort Ashby, and second because I knew in my heart that Dottie already loved him more than she loved me.

170

The longer we talked though, the more of a straight shooter Ronnie seemed to be. And Dottie wasn't a fool born yesterday and I had to trust her judgment. Not that a person uses too much judgment when she's busy being in love. Ronnie tried to include me in everything he said, which got a little strained after the first ten minutes. I wanted to tell him to just relax but you never know how someone is going to take a comment like that so I just kept nodding my head like some sort of half-wit and looking out the window a lot.

The music from the Bakery Warehouse was blasting when Ronnie's car pulled into the lot. You could tell Dottie was getting a little nervous about going public with Ronnie. She started talking a mile a minute, chattering on like a squirrel gone mad.

As soon as Ronnie got out to get our car door, I put my hand on Dottie's. "Relax. Everyone is going to like him just fine." That seemed to calm her down a bit. She just put her hand in his and let him lead her right up the side wooden steps and into the noisy crowd. I followed right behind, ready to wave to anyone who waved at me.

I was digging in my pocket for change to get a Coke when someone put their hands on my shoulders and spun me around like a top. "Hey there, Sugar!"

There stood Leroy Adams, a good six inches taller than when he left for college last September. His wrists looked as thick as telephone books as he locked them behind my neck. "Well, honey, haven't you gone and grown up nicely?"

His eyes grew large as he lowered them to my

chest. Leroy had always been a jerk, the kind of guy who thinks girls are just various sections of body all sewn together for staring. I pulled over Dottie and introduced Ronnie. I was hoping Leroy would go into his football glory stories the way he does whenever he meets someone who hasn't heard them all before.

But Leroy just nodded his head once in their direction and dragged me out to the dance floor. He wrapped his huge arms around my waist, just like they do on those bandstand shows, and started pulling me around the floor. Seemed every other step Leroy would wave to a friend and that friend would break in on us and ask me to dance. All of them held me tight, their sweaty hands making prints on the back of my dress. By the fifth song I had already danced with ten guys and I couldn't help but feel like the Queen of Sheba. Now I know darn well that I'm no Jessica LaShay so I was beginning to feel like there was a DANCE WITH ME PLEASE sign tacked on my back.

"Angel Baby" was playing and I was dancing with Leroy when I noticed Cody. He was leaning against the wall watching me. Linda Reeker and Meggie Kaines were flanking him like guards, laughing and touching his arms every other second, but it was me Cody was staring at above his Coke can. So even though I can't tolerate Leroy at all, I threw back my head and laughed like I thought he was a regular Johnny Carson. Let Cody think I was having a fine old time.

Cody scowled at me from across the floor, probably wishing he had let me drown all those years ago.

172

Leroy must have mistaken my laugh for something else 'cause his arm tightened around me, nearly snapping me in half. He put his lips close to my ear and whispered something in hot little breaths.

"What?" I asked, trying to pull away so I could at least read his lips.

"I said you have grown into quite the woman," repeated Leroy. He jerked me back to him and I felt suffocated by the swamp of flesh.

The music changed, going from slow to fast. But Leroy kept me locked to him, swaying more than moving to the music.

"I hear you learned to like older men this summer," whispered Leroy. His left hand slid down my back and squeezed my rear end. "Yeah, I hear you like them a lot, honey."

I tried to squirm out of his hold, but he grabbed the back of my dress and held me tight. "Relax, just enjoy it."

"Let me go, you idiot!" I put both hands on his shoulders and shoved as hard as I could. It was like trying to move a cement truck up a hill.

"I think it's time we took a little drive and got to know each other better," said Leroy. He licked his lips and put his hand around my neck. "Think you can teach a college boy a few tricks, Kitty?"

I kicked him in the shin and when his hands let go of me, I pushed him back. "Get away from me and stay away."

Leroy just grinned. "From a kitten to a wildcat, all in a summer. Cody was sure right about you."

"What do you mean?" I cried. But inside I think I already knew what he meant. Cody was telling all the guys what he thought about me and Mr. Curtis.

Leroy grabbed me again, rubbing his whiskered chin against my cheek. "So, are you ready to go?"

"Stop it," I shouted as he lifted me up in a giant bear hug.

Out of the corner of my eye I could see people turning around. A hand grabbed Leroy roughly on the shoulder, tearing us apart.

"Get away from her!"

Leroy turned, his fists up, an angry look on his face. It quickly turned to shock as a huge fist sailed toward him.

"Don't you ever touch her again!"

Cody's fist smashed against the side of Leroy's face. Blood squirted from his nose as Cody grabbed him up by the shirt and punched him again.

"Hey, cool off, man," said Ronnie. He grabbed Cody and pushed him back.

"Stay away from her!" The rage in Cody's voice scared me. Everything was happening too fast. I was shaking so hard I could barely stand. The violence in the air was as thick as heat. Everyone had stopped dancing now, pushing forward to get a closer look.

I shoved through the crowd, lifting my elbows to make a path. "Excuse me, excuse me, move, please."

"Kitty, Kitty Lee, wait." I could hear Cody's voice trailing me as I tried to get away.

He caught up with me by the refreshment stand, grabbing my upper arm and swinging me around to face him. "Are you all right? He didn't hurt you, did he?"

When I looked up at him, I could barely see his face, I was crying so hard. I wiped my cheeks, but the tears were coming so fast; as if an artery connecting the heart to the soul had been severed. I shook his hand free from me and clenched my fist, madder and more disappointed in him than I've ever been at another person in my life.

"I hate you, Cody Baines!" I shouted. "I'll never forgive you for your lies, never as long as I live."

I took a deep breath and I slapped him hard. And when I saw how shocked and hurt he looked, I hauled off and slapped him again.

Chapter Twenty-seven

I raced outside, clattering down the wooden steps and zigzagging through the parking lot. I never stopped running until I reached the dark grove of birch trees behind the Methodist church.

"Kitty Lee, wait!"

When I realized it was Dottie, I turned and walked back, meeting her at the edge of the parking lot.

"What in the world happened back there? Cody is threatening Leroy again and someone is calling the police."

"Good. Let them take Cody Baines to jail and throw away the key. He's been spreading awful lies about me, Dottie. I hate him so much."

Dottie reached in her pocket and handed me a tissue. "I thought it was nice of him to rescue you from Leroy. Why did you slap him?"

I sat down on the curb, wiping under each eye. "It's such a long story, Dottie. Do you think Ronnie will mind if the two of us just go back to my house and talk? I have so much to tell you."

Dottie glanced over her shoulder. Ronnie stood on the porch by the steps. He motioned to Dottie to come back inside.

"Gosh, Kitty. I can't. Ronnie and I were just about . . . tonight is kind of special."

I looked over at Ronnie, feeling jealous and left out.

"Can't he spare you for at least an hour? Lord, Dottie, you've been with him every day for weeks! You don't know half of what's been going on with me."

Dottie sat down next to me, scooping her full skirt around her knees. "I know and I've missed knowing." Dottie shrugged. "But you're so smart Kitty. You'll make sense out of everything; you always do." She put her hand on my knee. "Kitty, I want you to be the first to know our good news."

Looking up, I suddenly felt scared, like I already knew what she was going to say.

"Ronnie and I are eloping tonight. My bag is in the trunk. This time tomorrow I'll be Mrs. Ronald O'Brien."

My mouth fell open like a trap door. "Dottie, you can't. You're only sixteen!"

Dottie just smiled. "Seventeen next month. We're driving over to Delaware tonight."

My chest felt so tight I could hardly breathe. "Dottie, why?"

Dottie cocked her head and looked at me, a surprised look on her face. "Why? Well, because we love each other. That's all the why we need. Ronnie's job is finished here."

"But he can come back to visit," I reminded her. "You only have one more year of high school, Dottie."

Dottie stood up, brushing off her new dress. "I don't need another year of high school. All I need is Ronnie." She looked down and grinned at me. "You're my best friend. Aren't you even going to say congratulations?"

I stood up and saw Ronnie walking across the parking lot. My nose started tickling and I knew I was going to start crying any minute. I didn't want her to go. I didn't want to lose Dottie to Ronnie because I loved her, too, and I knew I'd never see her again. And even if I did, it would never be the same.

"Don't do it, Dottie."

Disappointment flashed in Dottie's eyes. She turned and reached out for Ronnie's hand as he walked up. "We'll write as soon as we get a place, won't we, hon?"

I just kept staring at Dottie. How could she leave her whole life here? How could she be that sure of Ronnie?

"Your mother is going to be so worried," I said quietly.

Dottie reached in her pocket and held up an envelope. "We're going to leave this in my mailbox for my mother. If she calls you, asking about me, tell her to read it."

I nodded, staring at Ronnie and Dottie. I knew a best friend should be hugging and kissing them right now. But I couldn't. I didn't want Dottie to go. I was scared for her. She was so young. I just reached out and touched her hand, then I turned and started walking fast. By the time I left the parking lot I started running, following the black iron fence past the church and cemetery and not stopping until I was deep in the woods where nobody could call out to me. By the time I followed the path by the creek and was walking up toward the clearing, the only sounds I could hear were the locusts and chickadees.

I walked for miles. The last time I heard the church bells it was ten o'clock. My feet were soaked from the dew on the grass, and I felt so lonely I put my arms around my shoulders and hugged myself tight. Loneliness was scary in big doses. It was kind of like black ink that could spill over everything, making even the good things gray and bleak-looking. Maybe what I was feeling could even get worse, could get so bad that you had to lock yourself away and lick your wounds.

I sat down on a rock, wondering if it was going to get worse. The longer I sat there, the more I knew that it wouldn't, that morning would burn off the darkest parts just as the sun always dried up the early fog.

I got up and started walking again. It seemed like a million years ago that Dottie, Cody, and I threw all our pencil stubs and half-used tablets away and charged down the front steps of Romney High School thinking that this summer was going to be the best.

I let my hand brush against the honeysuckle, wondering if I should just go and crawl onto Gramma Belle's lap like I used to after a hard day in elementary school.

"It will be okay," Gramma would say. "Just tell Gramma Belle what happened."

I leaned against a tree, hungry and miserable, wishing I was seven years old again. All of a sudden I looked around and realized where I was. I frowned, mad that my mind would trick me into Cody's backyard.

I hiked up my pink skirt and climbed up the ladder over the railing. Janice had stashed some of Gramma's oatmeal cookies up here this afternoon and I hoped they were still there.

I found the bag of cookies hidden in the hollow of a near dead oak. I leaned against the tree and ate the first three without stopping to take a breath. I had been so excited about the dance and meeting Ronnie, I had forgotten all about dinner.

I was holding the last cookie up to the moonlight, when I heard something below. Quicker than anything, I flattened myself to the floor of the tree house. In the daylight I don't believe the stories about Mr. Wessle coming back from the dead to pick up his mail, or that Mrs. Hawkins's husband finally did escape from prison and is headed back to kill as many ladies in Romney as he can find. But when the twigs start cracking and you're all alone in the dark, you start to rethink fears. Some sound a lot more credible in the dark.

"Damn that Kitty Lee Carter!"

"What?" I jumped up so fast I bumped my head on the railing. "Don't you dare damn me, Cody Baines!"

Cody jumped halfway up the ladder and glared right in my face. "Where have you been for the past two hours? They called the police, you know. I was just coming over to get the car and tell Gramma Belle you ran off before the sirens come shrieking up your driveway."

I crossed my arms and tried to look as unconcerned as possible. "Yes, and while you're there, be sure and tell Gramma Belle how you ruined my reputation by spreading rumors, downright lies, about me and Mr. Curtis."

I crumpled up the plastic bag and shot it right in his face. "Now please get off the ladder so I can go home."

Cody hopped over the railing and sat next to me. "For crying out loud, Kitty Lee, you've got to believe me. I never said a word about you and Mr. Curtis. Why would I mention it? It was killing me just thinking about the two of you together."

I shifted so I wouldn't have to look at Cody's face. "So who said we were together, anyway? I swear, Cody, you've known me all these years and you think I'd fool around with a married man?" I bit my lip, tasting blood. The kiss in the hospital hadn't been "planned" fooling around.

I felt Cody's arm on my shoulder. "Mr. Curtis *wanted* to be with you, Kitty. I could tell by the way he looked at you."

Truth was, Cody had seen something that really was there, that I didn't catch onto until the hospital. Maybe Mr. Curtis never even knew till it reached up and grabbed him.

"So then, why did Leroy say you were right, that I was interested in older men?"

Cody let his hand drop. "Hell, I don't know.

Some of the other guys started saying things. I told them it wasn't true, but they just kept jagging me, knowing they were making me mad."

I turned around. "So why were you mad? It was me they were talking about."

Cody stared at me a long time. Finally he just shook his head. "Can't you figure it out yet, Kitty? Everyone in town knows how I feel about you. They knew I was jealous. They knew I would kill anyone who tried to hurt you."

The tone of his voice almost stopped my heart. I had never heard it so gentle or caring before. The branches were blocking most of the moon, but even in the shadows it looked like Cody was ready to cry.

"Hey, Cody," I said, reaching out and taking his hand. "I guess I should have talked to you." I reached up and ran my fingers along his cheek. "Is this the cheek I slapped?"

Cody nodded. "Twice."

I could feel my cheeks blushing red, but I leaned over and kissed his cheek. A thin blanket of clouds blew over the moon, filtering a soft light over us both.

"Twice," whispered Cody again. He drew me close to him and kissed my neck. When he looked up, he held my face in his hands as he searched for something in my eyes. "I love you, Kitty Lee," he said. I kissed Cody first, reaching up and holding onto him like he might disappear. The second time Cody kissed me, and the third we were kissing each other. It was somewhere in the middle of that third kiss that I realized I loved Cody Baines.

Chapter Twenty-eight

Cody and I stayed in the tree house a long time. I told him a lot about the Curtis family. I told him all about Dottie running off with Ronnie. Cody just hugged me tight and kept listening. By the time we walked home, I was worn out with talking. I guess I didn't realize how much was piling up inside of me. The letting go felt good. I felt lighter and happier than I had in a long time.

"I love you," whispered Cody. He kissed me good-bye for the tenth time by the hedge.

"I love you, Cody." I turned back and grabbed his arm. "And if I hear you went back to that dance to make trouble, I'm going to be after you tomorrow." Cody pretended to look scared and we both laughed.

As I walked toward the porch, I could see the red glow from Pop's cigarette moving back and forth with the swing.

"Hi, Pop. You're up late tonight."

"Well, I slept most of the day." Pop leaned over and flung his cigarette out across the railing. "After watching you kiss Cody Baines like that, I'm beginning to think I should stay awake a little more often. No need to walk down to the Regent with carrying on like that going on by my front hedge." Pop chuckled. "I thought you were mad at him."

Right off I was surprised that Pop knew I had been mad at Cody. I guess Gramma had been updating him on my life whenever he woke up from his naps. "I stopped being mad."

"So I see."

We both laughed. I hopped up on the railing. "I've got more news, Pop. Once I stopped being mad, I realized I was in love."

"Just like that, huh?"

With the porch light off, I couldn't tell if Pop was in the mood to talk or not. But I was. "Was it that fast for you and Momma?"

For a few seconds, the only sound I heard was the squeaking of the porch swing. Then Pop sighed. "Yep, it was *that* fast. I saw her walking outside the high school one afternoon and I turned to my friend Eddie and said, 'See that pretty girl over there, Eddie? That's the girl I'm going to marry.' "

"And then you got married and had me." I was glad for the dark, hoping it would make talking easier. I sure didn't want to scare Pop off or pick at old wounds. But my whole life had been filled with things left unsaid. I was beginning to see that it was the unsaid things that caused the most festering and scarring.

"It's awful late, Kitten," said Pop. "You'd better get to bed if you have to work tomorrow."

"Gramma said she would go up to the Curtises' for me, Pop. I don't think I should spend so much time there." I waited for Pop to ask why, but he didn't. Maybe he sensed the answer. "Pop, Mrs. Curtis has a bad drinking problem. That's why Mr. Curtis needed so much help taking care of the kids."

"That so," said Pop. He wasn't one to pry into other people's affairs so he just busied himself with lighting another cigarette.

"She shuts herself up in the bedroom, calling it nerves." Pop was studying me through the thin blue smoke separating us. "She never combs Chrissy's hair, or helps Joey find his shoes, or . . . anything. She just stays in that bedroom, sipping whiskey with the door closed."

My chest was beginning to hurt. I was taking so much time so I wouldn't rush out with all my worries, that my vocal cords were locking up. I wanted to just lean close and ask Pop about Momma's problem. Why did she lock herself away from us?

"You know, there is a branch of A.A. down in Shanks," offered Pop. "I'll bet Mrs. Curtis could hitch a ride with Roy Coons if she felt funny about walking in alone. He wouldn't mind the company, I'm sure."

I wonder why Pop never thought to insist Momma ride down with Roy Coons so she could have gotten some help. I started swinging my feet through the railings. "Well, I don't see how she'll say yes to going. Mr. Curtis says his wife promises to kill herself if anyone tries to get her help."

Pop just shook his head, picking off bits of tobacco from his tongue. "She won't."

I leaned closer. Pop said it like he knew what he was talking about. "But how can you tell?" I wanted to know.

"I can, is all. Now tomorrow morning you call and tell Mr. Curtis to get her some help before it's too late."

I could barely swallow. Now was when Pop would turn to me and confide that no one ever got help for Momma and that's why she's not setting out here on the porch today.

"Look at that moon, Kitty."

I didn't even turn my head. I couldn't be bothered with the moon right now. I kept right on staring at Pop.

"Did Momma ever get help? Before she died?"

Pop sort of froze, looking up at the moon. I could see him swallow hard so I knew he was thinking deep on what I had just asked. He pitched his cigarette over the railing.

"No."

There, it was done. At last I knew. My body, perched on the railing, remained stock still. I wasn't mad at Momma. Just kind of sad for Pop and me.

"Nobody *could* help your momma," Pop said quietly. "It was that quick."

"Quick? How many weeks was she shut up in her room before she got into the car and ran off like she did?"

Pop leaned forward in the swing. "Just about two or three weeks . . ."

"Three weeks, Pop!" My eyes stung. "Couldn't you *make* her come out?"

Pop looked puzzled. "Hell no, I was the one who told her to stay in there."

"Why?" Maybe Momma's ragged nerves were too much for Pop to witness. Or maybe Pop didn't want Momma drinking whiskey from a jelly jar in front of people.

Pop got up off the swing and took a step toward me. "What's wrong, Kitty? Your momma had to stay off her feet because she was *pregnant* again and things weren't going right." Pop's eyes watered up. "I guess that's why I'm having such a hard time lately. The baby would have turned fourteen years old next week."

I nearly fell back in the Shasta daisies, that's how shocked I was. "Momma was pregnant?"

Pop nodded. "Yes."

"So Momma didn't drink?"

Pop laughed. "Drink? Your momma would get mad if I tried to slip anything in her eggnog at Christmas."

"And she didn't close her door on us?"

Pop put his hand on my shoulder. "Of course not. You were in that basket next to our bed half the time."

Tears started rolling down my cheeks, and when I looked up, Pop was rubbing at his eyes, too.

"I never knew she was pregnant. Why didn't you or Gramma tell me?"

Pop sighed. "We didn't tell anyone. Didn't want anyone to be sadder than they were already. I didn't want you thinking you lost a momma and a little brother or sister." A sad strangling sound came out of Pop's throat. "I miss her so much."

"I know you do, Pop. I guess that's why you've been sleeping so much and . . . and never talking about Momma, not even to me."

Pop's hand shook as he reached for another cigarette.

"You'd better start talking about it to somebody, Pop." I watched his face for a reaction. Pop frowned and shoved his cigarette back in his package.

"I'll be fine."

I slid onto the swing and wrapped Pop's arm around me. "Yeah, but if you don't get out of that bed more often, I won't be."

Pop's chest went up and down, breathing and thinking. Finally he gave my hand a squeeze.

"I'll help, Pop," I said quietly. "I'm a good listener."

Pop leaned over and kissed my forehead. "Too bad you can't just send problems off to a dry cleaners and have them come back on a Tuesday after five."

"Oh, don't I know it." I patted Pop's hand and sighed. "Boy, would we have run up a big bill this summer."

Pop laughed. "You make about as much sense as your momma always did." Pop reached down and messed up my hair. "The older you get, the more you act like her, Kitty." Pop's voice cracked and he just sat for a few minutes. "I guess that's about the nicest compliment I could ever give you," he finally said. Pop reached out for me and we hugged each other tight. I felt so much better. But I had to find out everything now, so I could finally put things to rest. "But if Momma had to stay off her feet, why did she get in the car that night to go up to the new mall?"

Pop grunted and you could tell he was still mad. "Because she was a stubborn Irishwoman, that's why. She was just starting to feel better and she got a sudden burst of energy. Your momma thought it was time she painted pink and yellow tulips on that wicker basket and let you put your doll babies in it. I offered to pick up the paint but she said that I would get all the wrong shades. She told me to just stay home and take care of you so she could get started on it before she had two babies to chase after.

"Then that furniture truck ran the red light and she was gone." We were both quiet, thinking of all the time we had been without her.

"But I know she's watching over us and . . ." Pop's voice cracked. "And selfish as it sounds, I'm glad she has that little baby to keep her company."

Pop clamped his mouth tight and looked straight at the moon like he half expected to see her up there. Tears spilled over his eyes and when I put my hand to my cheek, it was wet, too. Neither one of us reached up to wipe them away. Somehow Momma was part of them. I felt so close to Pop I knew we were going to be all right.

Pop reached out and pulled at the dried leaves of the morning glories. "Your momma loved these flowers."

I smiled and started helping him. "*And* your stories, Pop. I'm still waiting to hear some of them. Gramma said you were the best storyteller in Romney. Were you really that good?"

Pop hitched up his pants a notch and grinned. "Damn right."

I hopped back up on the railing and grinned back at Pop. "Well, if you were really that good, I'd appreciate it if you did me a real big favor."

"Sure, Kitten."

"Seems like Cody is going to be hanging around here for the rest of his life and I know we will have to listen to that story about him saving me from the Potomac *at least* another two hundred times. So I was thinking, it would be a whole lot nicer if you told him some of your stories and then he could repeat them. Will you help me?"

Pop started to laugh, a deep, rich laugh that I couldn't remember hearing in a long time.

"He could use some help, I'm sure."

"Who needs help?" asked Gramma from behind the screen door. She double-knotted her robe and came out on the porch. "Impossible to sleep when the porch is so noisy."

"Hi, Gramma. Cody is coming by tomorrow to ask you to marry him."

Gramma patted her curlers under her hair net, shooting me a sly look. "Good thing I just washed my hair."

She sat down in the swing and smoothed down the collar of her nightgown. "Course, after what I saw out by the hedge a few minutes ago, I don't think it's me Cody's after at all."

We all laughed, growing quiet and listening to

the sounds of the neighbors shutting up their houses. There wasn't a star or lightning bug out that night, nothing to rob the moon of its solitary glow. It drifted down on us, shining through the morning glory vines and splashing onto the porch, whitewashing us all. It was the most wondrous moon I could remember. The very brightest light.

About the Author

Colleen O'Shaughnessy McKenna began her writing career as a child, when she sent off a script for the *Bonanza* series. McKenna is best known for her popular Murphy series, the inspiration for which comes from her own family.

A former elementary school teacher, Ms. McKenna lives in Pittsburgh, Pennsylvania, with her husband and four children.

This is Ms. McKenna's first young-adult novel.